The Quartermaster

Adam Parish

*Book 1 of the
Jack Edwards and Amanda Barratt
Mystery series*

Also by Adam Parish
*Parthian Shot (2)
Loose Ends (3)*

To sign up for offer, updates
and find out more about Adam Parish
visit our website www.adam-parish.com

This is a work of fiction. Names, characters, organisations, places, events and incidents are either products of the author's imagination or are used factually.
Any resemblance to actual persons, living or dead, is purely co-incidental.

Text copyright @2021 by Adam Parish

No part of this book may be reproduced or stored in a retrieval system or transmitted in any form or by any means **(electronic, mechanical, photocopying, recording or otherwise)** without express permission.

ISBN 979-8-5950-8761-2

*Thanks to Helen
for her help,
humour,
and patience*

Chapter 1

McQueen had to yell to make himself heard above the noise of the sea and the wind. "Tell them to hurry," he rasped to the man at the head of the human chain snaking down the short beach.

The operation was proceeding well, but it was the sort of operation that made those involved feel that every minute was an hour and every hour a day. McQueen smoked incessantly as he nervously paced up and down the line, alternately urging care then speed.

He was a good manager. The haul was loaded in twenty-eight minutes, two minutes ahead of schedule. As his temporary assistants scattered, McQueen and two others jumped into the lorry and moved off slowly, using only the vehicle's side lights. The successful first stage set the pattern for the later ones and, despite the narrow roads, driving rain and the lack of lights, no difficulties were encountered on the short journey.

The lorry slowed and turned off the road onto a narrow track. The moon was full. "No lights," McQueen said.

This was a risk, but one he thought essential. Although the track was uneven and irregular, his driver had practised this exercise several times before. Even so, the drive had to be undertaken at a crawl, and it seemed like an eternity before the changing noise from the tyres told them that the journey was at an end.

McQueen leapt from the cabin, walked forward a few yards and cursed as he stumbled on irregular stones. His torch was powerful, and in a few paces he located the shaft entrance. He fiddled with the padlock and hauled back the heavy metal door. The passageway had been gouged through bare rock. It was damp and claustrophobic but only a few yards long, and it opened out into a small square general storage area and rough retreat. He reached into his bag, located the storm lamp and slung its cord over a well-placed rafter.

The retreat was adequately floored but partly and crudely panelled. McQueen observed a single, yellowing newspaper sheet pinned to the wall. The half-clad brunette smiled and seemed pleased to see him.

He noted with satisfaction that the debris on the shaft floor looked undisturbed, and after removing some he quickly located the steel ring. He bent over and tugged at it, the trapdoor lifting easily. As he stared down, all was dark except for the first of the wooden steps, and he turned and carefully placed himself on the top one and inched down into the blackness. At the bottom, he delved into his backpack and produced two further lamps from his bag.

This area was roughly the size of the upper area but was built to a higher specification. The walls were clad in solid brick with several areas further partitioned and the roof lined with metal. It was cold but it was free of damp. McQueen needed all these features.

He ascended the wooden stairs and went back outside. The lorry had concluded its manoeuvring and had halted with its rear doors a few feet from the shaft entrance.

The work was slow and awkward, and with only three people now it was many hours before the juggernaut had disgorged its cargo. When concluded, all trace of the men was removed. The trapdoor was closed, the covering debris replaced and the metal door and its padlock carefully restored.

The men returned to the lorry and again made the slow journey up the track without lights. This time, once on the main road, headlights were no longer a risk and, free of their cargo and their tension, the men sped away into the night.

Chapter 2

Through the narrow and barely adequate gap between her heavy lids, Kate Phillips caught sight of the bedside clock as the display changed from 6:58 to 6:59. She relapsed into her warm bed, determined to savour the remaining sixty seconds, probably the only part of this new day she would be able to call her own.

This would be an especially busy day, and Kate's mind, now well ahead of her still weary body, turned to planning the long hours ahead.

Her time was up. The clock buzzed and a newsreader's voice came through loud and clear. She was ready, and in ten minutes had showered, dressed, and - one piece of toast and a half a cup of coffee later - she was off.

Her daily commute was short and it was familiar, passing the little house where she had grown up – just her and her parents. She was forty-five now, older than either of them had been when they died. That was a long time ago, but she still missed them.

When they died, she had been inconsolable and even now, many years later, there was rarely a day when she didn't think of them. The grief had long gone, but in its wake was stronger and deeper residual emotion.

She turned into the empty car park and into a single space slightly larger than the others and nearest to the building's front door.

Acknowledging the security guard and eschewing the lift, she ascended two flights of stairs and walked down a narrow, deeply carpeted corridor, passing numerous deserted offices until, at its end, she reached the heavy, crafted oak door that bore her name: K. Phillips – Managing Director.

Her office was large, high-ceilinged and expensively fitted with a few old-fashioned furnishings, sparingly arranged. The small pile of centrally placed papers hardly did justice to the desk behind which she sat. She pulled them towards her and, having scanned and digested their prosaic contents, rose and passed through a door and into a smaller and less grand modern outer office.

Kate wasn't first in today. A young woman was on the telephone. "Wednesday morning at ten-thirty," she purred and then added firmly, "No, rearrangement is impossible." She replaced the receiver and looked up at Kate.

She was about thirty with great skin and sharp, well-arranged features. With her well-groomed thick brown hair, the overall effect was, if not beauty, something very close to it. She was tall, long-legged and curvaceous. Jane had, in her year at Struthers Bank, proved to be of powerful interest to many of her colleagues.

"Who was that?" Kate asked.

Jane's voice was deep, refined and cultured. "Mr Rowley. What a wanker."

Kate laughed.

"Coffee?"

"Please," Kate said. She took the cup and sat on the edge of Jane's desk. "What's on today?"

"Strategy meeting at 10:00, Smith from International at 11:30, lunch with Hopkins and his directors at 12:30 and then, although it wasn't easy, free for the rest of the day."

"Good. Bring me the last six-monthly financial summaries. And no calls."

Kate returned to her office and flicked idly through a newspaper. She had barely skimmed the front-page articles when Jane entered, placed the requested reports in front of her and left.

Kate pushed the newspaper aside and began studying the reports. As she did, she smiled as she recalled those siren voices who had issued dark warnings on the unsuitability of appointing a woman as head of the Struthers Private Bank.

And not only a woman, but a woman who had not followed the traditional routes of public school then Oxbridge. Far from it. She almost understood, even sympathised, with their pain at being comprehensively outplayed by their former copy typist. After her appointment, the vultures had found their diet to be a meagre one: improved profitability, lower costs and increased market share in every month since her appointment.

In normal commercial life, such improvements typically took time, but Kate had known what to do from the very first day. When rising through the ranks she had seen – and noted – every inefficiency and had, for years, been making herself indispensable. When she had, unexpectedly, been given the chance to implement her plans, she had not hesitated. And it had worked.

The bank was a relic of a long-gone past, as anachronistic as its small number of remaining customers. Established in the nineteenth century to service the needs of the Irish Ascendancy class, it had once been an important player in the British Imperial adventure. Now it was no more than a branch office of a multi-national bank, yet in every reorganisation its badge had been thought worth keeping – a decision that, in a modest way, had been justified. Struthers made a profit, and it had a risk profile that even the bank directors could understand.

As Kate digested the reports, she thought of the day ahead. The strategy meeting would be a bore – a typical blend of bluff, sycophancy and posturing, with the chance to hear her own ideas repackaged and then re-presented by others. She didn't resent that. There was a certain pleasure in the sight of middle-aged men, the same ones who for years had patronised and sometimes leered at her, now vying with each other for her favour.

She finished reading the reports and pushed them aside. After a moment's thought, she turned to her computer. Under the heading of "View Accounts" she passed swiftly through extensive security levels. LUNDY was entered, and she reviewed the information. She checked them all off. Only one was wrong: £200,000 wrong.

Ignoring the battery of telephones on her desk, she delved into her case and picked one from a selection of mobile phones. "Mr Littlejohn, please."

Chapter 3

At lunch, Kate refused another drink and suppressed a yawn. Hopkins Associates was exactly the type of client Struthers sought, and their acquisition represented a considerable success for Kate.

The lunch, however, had been overlong, the food mediocre and the attentions of the antique head of the company a bore. From the far side of the table an eager young executive was raising a glass in toast to the new association. Eager to escape the attentions of her unwanted admirer, Kate enthusiastically joined in, and, when they all drank and there followed a momentary silence, she seized the opportunity to suggest that the formalities begin.

The official signings were as brief as the lunch had been long, and - after once more deflecting a clammy hand en-route to her thigh - she rose and made her excuses.

She refused all offers of transport from her lunch companions and waited until they had all melted into the crowd, then she turned on her heel and walked against the flow of shoppers. At the end of the terrace of shops, she turned a corner, halted and looked around for a taxi. It was bitterly cold and she was in a hurry.

She was in luck. She jumped into the cab and gave the driver an address.

"You sure you want off here?"

"Yes, quite sure."

Ten minutes passed in silence before the cab pulled up alongside a large area of waste ground.

The driver had a last try. "Are you sure you want to get off here?"

She passed him a twenty-pound note and told him to keep the change, which settled the matter.

She stood for a minute and watched as the cab disappeared from sight. She pulled up the collar of her coat against a freshening wind and walked with her head low, passing first a row of depressing terraced houses and then some abandoned and graffitied factory buildings. A couple of youths kicking a football yelled something inaudible at her that she ignored. A few hundred yards later the locale improved – home to large Victorian villas and mature trees. At the end of the street she arrived at the entrance to the park.

She often came to this park to meet Peter. It was beautiful and peaceful. And it was empty. She followed the wide path through sweet-smelling evergreen trees until she reached their usual park bench, which was set some yards off the path and partially hidden.

It was a cold day, but she wasn't thinking about that. Her heart was beating fast, as it always did when she came here. She looked up and smiled involuntarily as she spied the black shape with the familiar swagger approaching. He was about thirty, tall and broadly built. His wild blond hair danced carefree across his handsome features, and his spivvy white trench coat flapped open as he approached. He stopped for a moment and peered through the trees then, slowly, walked towards her and flopped onto the bench. "Hello."

She leant into him. "Hello."

But his smile was gone, and he didn't look beautiful any more. He said sharply, "I hope this is important. As far as I know, everything's gone smoothly."

Kate moved away a little. "Yes, so far, although it seems to have cost us more than we expected."

Peter smiled. "Well, you know how it is, Kate. Extra money for greasing a few palms."

"Two hundred thousand pounds. That's a lot of palms."

Peter shrugged. "Czech customs people at the airport. Greedy bastards. Anyway, it's all fine. I've told you, it happens, there's no worries." He was impatient. "Is that all?"

Kate didn't say anything, and he smiled and moved nearer. She looked up. "Sorry, nerves getting the better of me."

He laughed and tossed back his golden mane. "Don't worry, darling, I'm right on the case. You know that." He was very close to her now. He wrapped his right arm around her neck and pulled her towards him.

She fell into the kiss and brought her own arm up on top of his. Her body quivered as his lips pressed against hers.

His body made a warm and comforting shield against the cold wind, and she tugged him towards her more intensely. With her free arm she reached down into her bag.

They needed air and broke off the embrace. He held her gaze and then moved forward to send her into ecstasy again.

Kate raised her arm and shot him in the head.

Chapter 4

That evening, Kate sat in her living room. The television blared. Peter's death was on the news. 'All the hallmarks of a contract killing . . . police investigating . . . major paramilitary groups deny involvement.'

Her book was more interesting. It wasn't complicated. He had deserved to die. No one was above the cause – *her* cause, the cause of so many others. His actions had threatened the cause. So, he had to die.

He had been an effective operative and not a bad lover, but he had become careless and stupid and, most annoyingly of all, he had underestimated her.

She knew Littlejohn hadn't asked for more money. Not that she believed a word Littlejohn said, but she had a well-placed, longstanding and reliable contact within his operation who had confirmed as much. Peter had taken the money.

She had, of course, always known about his expensive lifestyle and his even more expensive cocaine habit, but hitherto he had financed his activities by means of skimming revenues plus several private arrangements. But this time he had gone too far. She had covered for him in the past, but nothing could sit above her cause. She blamed herself a bit. She had trusted him once, maybe even loved him. There were still lessons to be learnt, even at her age, but there was no time to reflect on that now. She had more business to attend to.

She flicked off the television, threw aside her book, flung on a raincoat and stepped out into the night. The night was cold and wet, but her task was urgent. After a brisk walk of about five minutes, she arrived at the isolated building. These drinking clubs were no place for a woman of her age and social position, and she hiked her collar high up to shield her face as she hurried past the front entrance. She cut down the side of the building and then to the rear, stopping before a steel-lined door. The surrounding walls were daubed with graffiti and the cocktail of smells from the bags of rubbish and other loose debris was nauseating. She punched a code into a panel, and within seconds a slit in the door was drawn back.

Having satisfied the requirements of the voice from within, the slit snapped back and, a second later, the door was opened and she was admitted.

The back room of the club was small and spartan, lit only by a single unshaded bulb suspended by a threadbare cord over a central table and surrounding chairs. The walls were obscured by piles of beer barrels and the room smelt stale and musty.

She sat on one of the flimsy chairs. From beyond the adjoining door, she could hear the low noise of the club regulars. The man who admitted her stood silently alongside. She lit a cigarette, drew deeply and expelled the smoke in a long stream, illuminated as it passed through the narrow strip of light from the bulb. She did not look at him. "Get McQueen."

The man turned away, and a moment later another returned in his place.

The new man was short and fat and, although barely forty, was already bald. He was unshaven and wore an ill-fitting and badly cut pinstripe suit and a bright red shirt without a tie. He struggled into a seat opposite and helped himself to a cigarette.

Kate looked at him carefully. McQueen didn't look much, but he was her most able and most trusted colleague. Behind his shabbiness, only his piercing green eyes hinted at a keen and able brain. His appearance was a great help in their line of work. He was universally underestimated. And many were dead because of it.

McQueen was committed. Like Kate, he knew the importance of the cause.

"Did you see about Peter?" she asked.

"Yes, good riddance to the posing bastard. He won't be missed." It wasn't much of an obituary.

"So, everything's fine. When did you get back?"

"Aye, no problem at all, Kate. I got the last ferry last night."

"Any of our friends around?"

"No one I recognised."

Did you check out the goods?"

"Yes, I counted everything. Twice. I even tested a few of them. All good. Littlejohn did a great job."

"And what about here? How's that going?"

"We'll be ready within a month, not more."

"I wish it was quicker," Kate said.

"Yes, ideally, but everything's safe. We just need to hold our nerve."

Kate reached into her pocket and put the Glock on the table. "Get rid of that."

"You want a clean one?"

"Yes."

She waited as he retrieved a similar model from behind some barrels. She checked it thoroughly and put it in her pocket, after which she stubbed out her cigarette on the floor, returned home and went back to her book.

Chapter 5

On a high point of a bleak upland road, a long-lost wave of nostalgia overwhelmed Jack Edwards. In location and aspect the structure was unrivalled, but the years had been unkind to the house. Wild westerly winds with their salty cargo, compounded by years of neglect, had formed a deadly alliance and battered the sea-facing façade until it could stand no more, and it bore the indignity of abutting scaffolding like an ancient invalid.

His memory drifted back to better times. Balmy, everlasting summer days when he was young and life held no terrors. He thought of his aunt. Not incapable and ill-tempered as she had become, but a woman ahead of her time. A woman that defied the conventions of her age, snubbing and rejecting the demands of her class and gender, refusing to marry any of her many suitors, believing that to share her life with anyone meant compromise.

When her final and lengthy illness had begun, she had, however, cooperated with uncharacteristic acceptance. It was as if she had accepted that, by God's grace, she had enjoyed a more fulfilling life than anyone had a right to expect, and now it was payback time.

In her final days she had taken few steps to maintain the estate and had continually reduced staff numbers until, at the end, her only retainer had been her nurse. And it was only in the last month that she had contacted Jack and told him she would leave the entire estate to him. That was, if he wanted it.

He did want it. From the first, he had been certain that he should come here. True, that decision had been partly based on what he was currently doing. He still loved his subject – History and Economics – but didn't love the academic world with its petty jealousies and tiresome intellectual posing by colleagues. The chance to escape that world could not be passed up. And then there was the money. A lot of it.

He cautioned himself by recalling the words of his late aunt about the challenges and responsibilities that accompanied life in a rural outpost. "The deeds might be in your name, but remember – you're a trustee."

Jack thought he knew what she meant.

Whether this new arrangement would suit Marion, he didn't know. Loyal, supportive, and endlessly resilient, she sat alongside.

She yawned and flicked her long dark hair off her face. "How far now?"

"Five, maybe ten minutes."

She stretched her legs and shut her eyes.

Jack looked at her. She looked younger than her thirty-six years and a lot younger than he did, as a glance in the rear-view mirror confirmed.

She looked happy and relaxed. He knew she would adapt, but would she be happy? They had been together nearly ten years and she had agreed to come with him without much deliberation. That was unusual for her. She was a city lawyer who invariably questioned everything. But not this time. Maybe she just loved him?

The baronial house came back into view. He nudged her. "Well, what do you think?"

She smiled across at him and touched his arm. "I'll get used to it."

The approach road that hugged the headland narrowed and the 4x4 was having difficulty in overcoming the light snow covering. It was a relief when he finally turned into the driveway of the house with its holding gravel.

The car door extended violently as the force of the wind hit it squarely and Jack dashed to the outer defending door of the house. The sleet was relentless and he conducted a frantic search within his coat for the well-stocked ring of keys. Having tried most of them, the last one succeeded in shifting the lock. The massive wooden door, however, had evidently not been opened for some time and refused to yield to his promptings.

Frustrated, wet and cursing freely, Jack drove his shoulder against the door. He recoiled, and his shoulder stung with pain. The sleet blew into his face. He took a step back, and the sole of his boot provided an answer.

He entered into the blackness of a vestibule. He stumbled as he walked into something, and then managed three careful strides until he stood before an inner door. A speculative grope along the wall located a switch and then there was light. No longer pressured by the driving sleet, he selected the right key at his first attempt.

He passed through the door, entered the hall and switched on a light to reveal a familiar sight.

Marion was now alongside. She shivered. "This place is freezing."

"Yes, let's get our stuff in quickly and then explore."

This exercise took a few minutes. Jack slammed the outer door shut and they stood close. He put his arm over her shoulder and pulled her near. She smiled and he smiled back as they surveyed their new home.

Chapter 6

Jack and Marion slept late. In spite of the lateness of the hour, at this time of year – at fifty-eight degrees latitude – it was only just first light. Jack struggled to the bay window and heaved back the heavy curtains.

It wasn't a bad morning, and it was a stunning view. The storm had moved on to menace other parts and all outside was calm and clear. The sheer cliffs that encircled the bay, home only to the seabirds, stood noble and grand. He began to think of the forces that had, by their random application, produced this triumph, but he hadn't found an answer when his musings were cut short by a shrill ringing, which brought him back to the modern world.

Not quite the modern world. Who used a landline these days?

Marion stirred and Jack swore. The phone was deafening and couldn't be ignored.

"Hello?"

"Morning, Jack," a voice boomed. David Simmons, Jack's publisher. Simmons continued, "Sorry to knock you at this time but thing is, old boy, we've all been terribly patient, but it's now more than three months late."

"How did you get this number?"

"Never mind that. The good news is that help is at hand. I know that all the research is complete, so I've sent Amanda up. She'll have everything ordered in no time. Very efficient, Amanda."

Jack grunted. "I'll need a few days."

"Well, I put her on yesterday's late flight to Glasgow. That's in Scotland, yes?"

In the face of such amiable ignorance, Jack's irritation gave way to amusement. "Yes, Glasgow is in Scotland." He added, "And about three hundred miles and five hours away from Mascar."

Such minor geographical difficulties proved no barrier to Simmons' plans and he merely averred, "Oh well, I expect she'll find you."

Jack tried a final limp appeal. "Hang on, David, I've just moved house. Can't you give me a few more weeks?"

"Can't do that, old man. Be nice to Amanda now. Cheerio."

Jack cursed at the now-dead phone. He had known Simmons for years and, annoyingly, he was right. Jack had been putting off revising his first draft for months, and nothing short of a kick up the backside would work.

With his dramatic change in fortunes, he had considered abandoning the project. Who cared about monetary policy in the Weimar Republic? But somehow he didn't feel able to let Simmons down. He had promised him the book, and the £10,000 advance had been undeserved and very welcome at the time.

He knew Amanda and he liked her, and so did Marion. They were old friends. He also knew her efficiency. Simmons was right about this.

Jack considered going back to bed, but the shafts of sunlight outside were enough to dissuade him. He quietly slipped on jeans, a pullover and an overcoat and went out of the front door.

The wind was lighter and the day marginally warmer than he had imagined, and all trace of last night's thin covering of snow had gone. He passed from the gravel drive onto the single-track road that had given him so much trouble the previous evening. At its head, the track branched right and left. He headed right and began the steep descent to the village.

It was only a short walk to the village – less than a mile – and in fifteen minutes he had arrived at the first of its few buildings. The village was at sea level and consisted of a single street with buildings on his left and a small sea wall no more than two feet high on his right.

The adequacy or otherwise of the wall was not, however, currently being tested as the tide was out, exposing miles of brown rocks with their weed-covered bunting.

A huge white gable wall announced the Mascar Hotel, the largest and, more importantly, only licensed outlet for many miles. Unusually, the hotel was owned by natives of Mascar. He looked at the licence plate above the door and saw that they were still at the helm.

From what he remembered, the McAllisters ran a relaxed establishment, rarely observing standard licensing hours. As the nearest policeman was one of the hotel's best customers, this flexible policy was rarely challenged. As Jack passed the main entrance and peered through the open door into the abutting public bar, he saw that it already contained two drinkers. He hesitated. It was early, just after ten. Still, what the hell . . . He strode in.

The linoleum-covered floor was red and shiny and the bar smelled more of cleaning fluid than liquor. At the far end of the bar two drinkers were in deep conversation with a barman. Jack sat on a bar stool and waited. More than a minute passed before the barman, no longer able to maintain the pretence of not having noticed him, shrugged and approached him.

The message was disappointing and as short as the wait had been long. "We're closed," he announced.

Jack was too experienced – and now too thirsty – to be satisfied with such a blatant absurdity but said nothing, merely casting an exaggerated look across to the two drinkers. The barman slowly turned to follow his gaze but smiled self-assuredly. "Sorry, sir, these gentlemen are residents."

Jack had a quick word with himself. He didn't really need a drink, so he decided to accept this lie. He turned on his heel but he didn't get far. An older man emerged from behind the gantry and looked at Jack. "Mr Edwards?"

"Yes."

The man turned to the barman. "All right, Keith, I'll attend to this." The barman seemed a little disappointed at the removal of his opportunity to exercise authority, shrugged again sullenly and re-joined the conference at the far end of the bar.

The newcomer extended a hand. "Jim McAllister."

Jack shook his hand. McAllister was a large, round man of about fifty. He was clean-shaven with a florid and cracked complexion. It was the face of a man who enjoyed his work. Without speaking, he turned to the gantry, lifted two glasses and pressed each of them twice against the optic. He came out from the bar and sat down next to Jack.

To Jack's knowledge, he had met McAllister only once before, over five years ago, and that meeting had been brief. He was surprised McAllister remembered him. But no doubt news of his arrival was common knowledge.

After two long draughts of the spirit, McAllister ventured, "A big change for you?"

"Yes", Jack replied and added, "That's part of the attraction, but there's quite a lot to do . . . The house and the outbuildings. They need some repairs. Is there anyone locally?"

McAllister indicated the two drinkers at the other end of the bar. Jack eyed them and turned back to McAllister, who accurately read Jack's expression and defended his choice. "Oh, you won't usually find them in here at this time of the day, but since the quarry closed, work's been scarce."

The quarry. Jack had wondered how long it would be before it came up. At its peak, sometime in the 1970s, it had employed many hundreds, but changing tastes and a persistent failure to reinvest had caused a steady decline. But it was important locally, so, with a typical sense of duty, and despite mounting losses, his aunt had kept the quarry going through the declining years. She had ignored the protests of some advisers, firmly telling them that her family had provided local employment for nearly a century and would continue to do so as long as she was alive. Her long decline had eventually taken matters out of her hands, and the quarry had died with her.

Jack knew that with his arrival there would be hopes the quarry might reopen. Annoyingly, and unlike most of those interested, he knew that this was, in theory, a viable course. Prior to his arrival, he had studied a selection of the latest survey reports. They had shown that, with investment, many years of further reserves were available.

But Jack did not want to reopen the quarry. His aunt's money meant that he need never work again and this was his firm intention. But he knew that conscience would reproach him, and every day as he moved among the locals he would know that it was within his power to improve their lives. He had hoped to put off this inner fight for as long as possible, but it had already started.

McAllister continued dolefully, "Not just the quarry, of course, but we're down to only a couple of boats these days."

"Boats?"

"Aye, the harbour up the road. Used to be about thirty in the fleet. Now with quotas and Eastern European factory ships . . . They could drink, could the fishermen."

Jack took a long mouthful of the malt. Bugger the quarry. He finished his drink. He wanted another but didn't want to talk about the quarry, so he refused McAllister's offer.

He emerged onto the main street and continued exploring. Not that there was much to explore. Half a dozen white two-storey terraced houses. The last of them was a little bigger than the others and had been converted into a small general store. Jack and Marion were out of virtually everything, so he went in. A bell above the door rang, which alerted a middle-aged woman who emerged from behind a curtain.

"Hello, can I help?" she asked in a standard Home Counties accent.

"Yes, I've just moved in up the hill, and—"

"Oh, you must be Mr Edwards!"

He admitted as much and, without enthusiasm, proffered his hand to meet hers.

Ms Alison Crawford could certainly talk. He learnt that she had quit the rat race and a position pretty high up in the advertising world three years ago. About this decision she seemed to have few doubts, and she enthused about her new life, although Jack noted that the eulogy was peppered with disapproving comments on local practices, with accompanying suggestions for improvement.

Jack listened politely but already he knew that she would not be popular.

She was still talking. It was slightly alarming: she seemed to know an unnerving amount about him. Discussions on his coming had evidently not been confined to the public bar of the hotel – a place he felt sure Miss Crawford would not patronise.

She gushed on and so there he stood. A local curiosity. It was a part he had no choice but to play, and in a way, it wasn't unfair. If others had done him the honour of talking about him, he should, he supposed, at least be sufficiently gracious to present himself and allow them to test and measure him against their expectations.

"And of course," she said, "things are very quiet at this time of year without the tourists. And there's so little work for the tradesmen since the quarry shut."

Jack nodded and smiled weakly.

At last she stopped to draw breath and he seized his chance. Remembering the list he had compiled with Marion the previous evening, he produced it from his pocket.

She took the list from him, scanned it and looked up and began commenting on each entry. "Yes, yes, no, Friday, no."

Midway through this review she produced a small stepladder and reached to a top shelf in search of a little-requested item. In spite of her ill-fitting corduroy trousers, her ancient wool sweater and her mass of disorganised red hair, she had a decent figure, was not unattractive and was probably nearer thirty than forty.

As she came down from the step she began again. "As for the community council, they're living in the dark ages. I mean, who hasn't got a Facebook page these days?"

"Me, actually," Jack interjected.

"Well, I told them that I would set it up and run the whole thing. Nowadays a digital presence can do so much for a community. But they weren't interested. Can you believe that?"

"Yes, oh I mean no, no," Jack stammered. "Very short-sighted of them."

Crawford seemed satisfied with this answer. "Well, I'm sure I can count on your support. I'm determined to raise this again."

"I bet you are," Jack mumbled.

"What's that?"

"Quite right. Oh, and what time do you close? We're going to need quite a lot more stuff I think."

"Our winter hours are eight to three thirty"

"Okay. Well, I must be going. So much to do."

"Yes, I'm sure you have," Crawford said sadly.

Chapter 7

Once outside, Jack sat on the sea wall. The distant noise of the sea and the calling of the gulls were soothing to his spinning brain after the bombardment from the loquacious shopkeeper.

The peace was again cut short by a screech of tyres and a growl from a powerful engine from the far end of the village. By the time he had turned around, the car was beside him. The window slid down. "Good morning, Mr Edwards," came another Home Counties accent.

"Hello, Amanda." He fell into the vehicle. "Nice car."

"Yes, I had to use a bit of leverage at the airport. They mucked up my reservation, but it wasn't a problem, given my ex-husband owns the rental firm."

"Ex-husband?"

"Yes, the divorce was finalised a few months ago. I'm a free woman now."

"And a wealthy one?"

Amanda laughed. "Well, James never minded about money." She turned and looked at Jack. "Jeez, Jack, you might have dressed for my arrival."

"I do my best," he said defiantly. "How are you?"

"Good."

And she looked good, he thought. Piercing blue eyes weren't meant to work for brunettes, but everything worked for Amanda.

"So, what do you think of Scotland?"

"Not much. First time I've been here. Lashing rain, freezing, and rotten roads. You're not going to spend all your time here, are you?"

"Well, it's better in the summer, but I think I'm going to stay here." Jack was serious. "It's as close to a home as I've got."

Amanda raised her brows. "Hmm. Anyway, how's the book coming on?"

"Slow."

"Well, we'll soon sort that out. How's Marion?"

"Fine, she's looking forward to seeing you."

"Well, she won't be seeing much of you. We need that book."

"We just arrived yesterday," Jack protested.

"Well, you promised us the book three months ago." She revved the car. "Right, where's this house of yours?"

"Just up the hill, then first left."

He held on tight to the car door handle as she sped up the hill and pulled into the drive, scattering gravel everywhere.

Chapter 8

Jack had been hoping that Marion and Amanda would spend a lot of time catching up on university days and leave him alone. He really couldn't work up any enthusiasm for the book. That was a previous life. So far so good: the women were engaged in easy conversation about potential alterations to the house.

Jack, meanwhile, took refuge in a slow perusal of yesterday's London evening paper that Amanda had brought with her. The events reported seemed a million miles away, and Jack considered with detached interest the editorial comment on the likelihood of renewed disruption to the capital's Tube service. He couldn't care less about London transport – and that felt good. This turned out to be the same for almost everything else in the paper and he threw it down.

"I've got a couple of people to see today," he announced. "Could we make today a free day and start on the book tomorrow?"

Amanda considered this request. "Yes, why not? Marion and I need to catch up, but one day only."

This agreed, Jack excused himself and headed for the ground-floor study. It was a large room. The walls seemed to be made of books, and there were two desks, each supported by only a single chair. The larger of the two desks was crude, sturdy and strictly functional – the sort of reassuring desk that allowed anyone to put a hot coffee cup on top of it without any feelings of guilt. The smaller of the desks was sited at a large bay window and, as the study was to the rear of the house, it allowed for spectacular and uninterrupted views of the uplands and their craggy tops.

Jack sat at the large sturdy desk. It felt like his study.

Both sides of the desk contained large drawers, and Jack, with nothing better to do, delved into the first one. His aunt had a lot of business interests and a lot of money, and that generated a lot of paperwork, but this drawer was devoted only to the quarry.

Jack sighed, but this seemed like a good time to get up to speed. He retrieved a large bundle of documents and began a desultory review. It soon became clear that the quarry had been a much larger operation than he had imagined. More than a hundred employed as recently as five years ago with profits and then losses measured in millions of pounds. In Mascar, that represented a game-changing enterprise for the local community. No wonder it had been already mentioned.

Even closure had not reduced the volume of correspondence, and production reports were now replaced by submissions from a variety of groups bidding for the right to take over the operation. There were a number of offers ranging from proposals to operate under licence to outright purchase of the land.

As he reached the end of a voluminous file, it was clear that some of these offers were still open, even a year after closure. Time after time, advisers, mostly a lawyer called Mr Sutherland, had sought a decision from his aunt, but there were none of the short annotations against the letters. On the other hand, proposals to sell off the land had not met with her approval, and these offer documents were sprinkled with salty marginal phrases of rejection, untypical from the pen of a respectable elderly spinster.

And then the correspondence abruptly ended.

Jack rocked back a little in his chair. His aunt had been right. She was gone but he was here, and the letters would surely restart.

Maybe he could get in front of things? He picked up a few of the proposals and gave them a more thorough read. It was quickly clear that there was a great deal of potential for further development of the quarry. Every surveyor's report indicated that the immediately adjacent area had reserves enough for many years of full-time production. As Jack read on, it became increasingly apparent that the commercial case for some sort of development was overwhelming, and it was only the form of the commercial arrangement that was under discussion. Available markets existed, both at home and abroad, prices (both current and forecast) were high and there was an abundance of local skilled labour.

Jack put down the last of the proposals and put his head in his hands. It was so depressing. He wanted a quiet life. He didn't want to take any more decisions, especially decisions about people and money. He picked up the document again, this time focusing on difficulties, risks or something he could cling to, but there was nothing substantive. Even political activists were a let-down. It seemed that every group and organisation within a hundred miles was in favour of redevelopment, and many had taken the trouble to write to that effect. There were no bats or toads, and even the local environmental activists had offered no objection. Apparently local stone was better for the new low-carbon economy, whatever that was.

Of course, Jack could simply ignore it all, but he doubted he would have the willpower or the selfishness to resist the coming clamour.

The Quartermaster

He replaced the papers untidily and sought relief in the other drawer. It was less crammed and contained a selection of neatly arranged files which covered a range of financial and other estate business. The banking and investment records were more enjoyable. A file such as this was a revelation to Jack. The papers were perfectly ordered, and all communications from the bank were couched in tones utterly unfamiliar to him. Not a single letter expressed regret about being unable to honour a cheque or requested that additional funds be lodged to meet forthcoming debits.

The monthly report from the bank to his aunt was almost grovelling in tone, thanking her for her valued custom and assuring her that if there was ever anything they could do, she need only ask.

He was wealthy now and it felt strange. Noting with amusement that his aunt's bankers were also his own, he determined that he would have some fun at their expense when the opportunity arose.

The source of his aunt's income had been primarily from investments, although he was surprised to learn how extensive her interests had been within the village itself. In addition to the rental income from more than two dozen farms within the area, she owned about half of the houses within the main street and, Jack was interested to note, a half share in the Mascar Hotel. This arrangement had arisen about five years ago in consequence of the granting of a large loan, apparently for essential repairs to the building.

As he delved further into the drawer, he established that, in addition to being entitled to one half of the realised sum from any sale, the estate was to receive a monthly share of the hotel's profits. From the records, it was clear that McAllister was many months in arrears with these payments.

Adam Parish

He couldn't read any more. He poured himself a large bourbon. There were too many responsibilities, and his hopes of an idle and desultory life were fading fast.

Chapter 9

Some weeks ago – after, admittedly, promptings from Marion – Jack had made appointments with both his aunt's solicitor and her accountant. Today he regretted those actions and was tempted to cancel, but he really didn't have much of an excuse. Besides, he couldn't leave Marion to do everything. This professional duo were based in Inverness, about an hour's drive away. It was an enjoyable journey and gave Jack the chance to enjoy the hills and lochans and an occasional flying raptor.

His first meeting was with Mr Sutherland, a partner in Messrs Tainsh, Bell & Company Solicitors. The office was a little way outside the city centre and parking was easy. It was a surprisingly modern foyer into which he entered and, after a brief word with the receptionist, he sat and waited. Within the artificial jungle, Jack struggled to choose between local property guides and the variety of investment journals. He selected one of the latter, and just as he felt that he was on the point of a breakthrough in the understanding of unit trust schemes, he was interrupted by the receptionist.

A moment later he was sitting in a low, green leather armchair with a massive over-polished mahogany desk in front of him. Behind this magnificent structure sat a man who hardly did it justice. Sutherland was younger than Jack had imagined – maybe thirty-five. A little younger than Jack himself. Did he himself look that old?

Sutherland was a small man and his hair was mostly grey. He wore a standard business-class pinstripe uniform and sensible pair of glasses, but for all this appeared to fall short of achieving the level of gravitas Jack expected of a provincial lawyer. When Sutherland opened his mouth, this impression was reinforced; his utterances were delivered in high, nervous tones and at a speed which suggested that he was late for another, more important, appointment.

"We've a lot to cover, Mr Edwards. Shall we get cracking?"

"Yes, suits me."

By way of accompaniment to his speech, Sutherland threw in an impressive range of nervous gestures, the most prominent and regular being the continual removing and replacing of his glasses. Why was Sutherland so highly strung?

Engaged in these speculations, Jack suddenly looked up. His gaze was met by the lawyer with a mouth that was firmly closed. Jack had not listened to a word the lawyer had said. He returned the gaze and looked at Sutherland quizzically. Maybe Sutherland would repeat the question.

He didn't.

"Yes, yes, of course," Jack observed blandly. This didn't draw Sutherland either so he launched into his own speech. Whether it in any way related to what Sutherland had said, he could not be sure.

"Mr Sutherland," Jack said deliberately and confidently – well, it *was* his money, "I understand that you had full power over my aunt's business affairs and I would like you to continue to exercise this responsibility for, say, another month, or at least until I have finished my current book and got my feet under the table."

"Very well, Mr Edwards."

The Quartermaster

Jack continued, "Just keep things as they are. For example, no decision will be made on the future of the quarry until I have had a chance to consider the matter further. As I understand it, there are a number of proposals on the table and I want to review them all."

Sutherland removed his glasses. "The quarry proposals may be withdrawn unless a decision is made soon. They are both conditional on work starting this spring. In practical terms, this requires an early decision. Any further delay would be disastrous and may involve you in a great deal of expense."

Jack suppressed a smile.

"The existing buildings, plant and machinery are still largely functional and would, of course, be taken over by either of the consortia; however, should this plant become unusable you would be legally obliged to dispose of it. Any subsequent bids if, indeed, there were any, will be of a significantly lower amount. Now, as I see it, the Thompson Group's bid is by far the best."

Jack's head was spinning. What Sutherland was saying was all good sense, no doubt, but he was not in the mood for a full-blown conference today. No doubt Sutherland would give him the best advice, but already he did not care for the man.

"Yes, I can see all that," Jack interrupted. "Maybe we can talk in a week."

Sutherland closed his folder. "All right, we will reconvene in a week."

Jack rose, but before he could make a move for the door, the lawyer was round from behind the desk with a bundle of papers. "These orders need to be signed," he said. "Instructions for on-going maintenance and repair work to various properties, plus authority to transfer the necessary funds to cover such work."

Jack skimmed each of the papers within the bundle and scrawled his signature flamboyantly where indicated. When he had finished, he shook hands with Sutherland.

"Same time next Friday, then?" Jack enquired.

"Yes."

Jack left the office, determined that he would break the habit of a lifetime and get to grips with his affairs. Arguing with Sutherland for the rest of his life was a pleasure he would prefer to forego.

After enquiring of a passer-by, Jack decided that he would leave the car. As directed, a short walk took him to the offices of Brown & Henderson Limited.

The offices were as well-appointed as those of the lawyers. He sat and waited for a few minutes, reading ubiquitous and uninteresting magazines.

A young man emerged. "Mr Edwards?"

"Yes."

"Mr Brown will see you now."

If the reception areas were similar, the office he was led into was very different. Where the legal office had been traditional, this one was thoroughly modern, containing a selection of unprepossessing furniture, a modest desk and central table. An array of computer terminals and peripherals lined the far side of the room.

His host was an even greater contrast. Hamish Brown was a tall and well-built man of about forty-five with a shock of ill-cared-for dark hair and a beard that was out of control. He also wore the regulation pinstripe suit with an unadventurous tie, but he looked ill-at-ease so dressed, the sort of man who would look untidy whatever he wore.

Brown rose immediately from behind his desk and ushered Jack to the central table, shaking him warmly by the hand.

"Good afternoon, Mr Edwards," he enthused. "Hamish Brown. Please call me Hamish."

Brown sat and, looking at his watch and then at Jack, and apparently satisfying himself that there would be no breach of protocol or wounded sensibilities, said, "Drink?"

Much better.

Brown leaned over from his seat to a small, free-standing cabinet, and after a short search in the lower drawer produced a bottle of malt and two massive tumblers which he placed on the table and proceeded to fill liberally.

"Cheers," said Brown. "Welcome to the Highlands." From one of his jacket pockets Brown produced a packet of cigarettes and tossed them onto the table.

Smoking in an office had been illegal for more than a decade. Brown extracted an untipped cigarette and lit it. "Want one?"

Jack laughed. "Yes, I will."

"Well, how are you settling in?" asked Brown. "Lovely village, Mascar. I often go there to walk the hills. Good fishing as well round at the point. Do you know, I still hold the record for the biggest sea bass caught in the district?"

"No, I didn't know that. Actually, I don't fish."

Brown exhaled a plume of smoke. "Pity."

"I do a good bit of walking. Or at least I used to. I'm a bit out of shape."

"That's good."

Jack was warming to this unconventional adviser. "Maybe you would like to come over some time and guide me around the place?"

"Delighted," Brown replied. "In fact, I was thinking of taking tomorrow off. The weather forecast's good. How would that suit you?"

"Why not?" Jack replied.

The accountant continued, "We could knock off the two hills at the back of your place and then a couple of pints at McAllister's."

Jack had barely started on the malt and Brown was refilling his glass. Jack was already looking forward to tomorrow.

Brown unexpectedly switched to business. "You know, of course, that Sutherland handled all of your aunt's affairs. We only do the annual accounts and a few other ad-hoc things."

"Weren't you involved in preparing plans and projections for the quarry?"

"Yes, a few. Have you bothered to read any of them?"

Jack said, "Yes, I've skimmed a few," and admitted, "but not in any great depth. They all seem very positive."

Brown looked at him closely. "Are you?"

"No, not really. To be honest, I had this vision of coming up here and, well, doing not much, but it doesn't look like it. I've only been up here a day and about three folks have mentioned the quarry."

He had known Brown only about ten minutes but already felt that he could confide in him. "To tell you the truth, I can't be bothered with this quarry business. It's a damned pest, but it seems I can't avoid it."

Hamish sympathised. "Yes, I know. It could create jobs, but do you want the hassle?"

"Are you in favour?"

Brown lit another cigarette from the remains of the last and said, "All the financial projections look okay, but there's always risk with any venture. Look, you don't need to decide now, just get settled in."

Jack persisted. "Yes, I know that, but are you in favour?"

"As an accountant, possibly, but as a local, not so much. It changes the character of the area. Makes it too dependent on a single source of employment and when it closes, then what? I'm afraid I'm rather an old romantic. I like to think of people living on the land, hunting and fishing, all that sort of thing. Of course, I've no right to this opinion. I make my living from others' industry and commerce." He paused, then added, "But these are not real objections. Anyway, you've got plenty time to work out what you want to do."

"True enough, but I can't help thinking that I'll have to open the damn thing. If I live in the community, as I intend to, how will I be able to look everyone in the eye, knowing that my selfishness was impoverishing them? And besides, my aunt was a great one for responsibilities. Noblesse oblige and all that. The bloody annoying thing is that I already feel as if I've lost control over the entire decision."

"You're a wealthy man now," Brown said. "Get used to it. You decide on the timetable."

Jack smiled weakly. This was true, but it didn't feel as comfortable as he thought it would be. He was tired of business now and returned to hill walking. As he rose to leave, he said, "See you tomorrow then?"

"Yes, I'll come over about 11:30."

When Jack looked back as he left, Brown was taking another long drag of his cigarette.

Chapter 10

When Jack returned to the house dusk was already falling but, in contrast to the previous evening, the house was now reassuringly bathed in light. He had been there only two days, but tonight he felt the comforting feeling of having returned home.

As he entered the house the heat and the food smells hit him and he followed them into the kitchen. Inside he found Marion with her back to him, giving attention to a number of pots atop the Aga. He came up behind her, enveloped her in his arms and began to kiss her neck. She responded affectionately and pressed herself back towards him.

"How was your day?" Jack asked.

"Fine. We walked down to the beach and then for miles around the headland. It's so beautiful."

"Yes, it is," he replied softly.

They were very close. Jack moved his hands up from her tiny waist and slipped them inside her pullover. She wasn't wearing much underneath and Jack's hands were wandering a bit, but whatever he had in mind, his high passion was suddenly quelled by a shout from behind.

"Hello, you two!" Amanda blasted. "Is the supper ready yet? I'm starved."

Jack jerked his head around, dropping Marion's pullover, and acknowledged Amanda meekly.

If Amanda felt any awkwardness or embarrassment, she did not show it. She sat at the table, picked up a wine bottle and helped herself to a large glass.

Marion returned her attention to the pots, which left Jack standing feeling unreasonably self-conscious. He threw himself into, at least for him, frenzied activity and located and set place mats, poured glasses of wine for himself and Marion, made a half-hearted attempt at locating cutlery and then slumped, exhausted, at the table.

He leant back in his chair. He was tired and he could not imagine why. Compared with a working day during the university term he had done very little, but those days had been sustained by endless cigarettes, black coffee and alcohol. He was off this merry-go-round now, and it seemed that years of over-exertion had overtaken him. The close comfortable heat in the kitchen pressed heavily on his eyelids and he fell into a light sleep.

All too early, Jack was awoken as Marion sought space on the table for the assortment of bowls and pots. He was ravenous, having not eaten all day, but was still resentful at the interruption to his sleep. However, the stew within the largest pot tasted as good as it looked and the feeling passed. All three ate heartily and there was no attempt at small talk.

It was not until they had finished that the silence was broken by Amanda. "Jack, we should make a start on the book tonight."

Jack stretched and yawned.

"Just a quick look over the papers to get them in order. Can we set aside a few hours?"

Jack looked across at Marion. Maybe she would have some objection. But she said, "Why not? I could look over some of those estate papers for you, and I'd like to have a nose through the books in the study."

Jack, having failed to elicit the excuse he sought, conceded. "Yes, okay, we'll get cleared up in here and then I'll need to get cleaned up. Say about seven?"

Chapter 11

Although it was after eight, Kate Philips was still at her desk. She closed the file and placed it on the right-hand side of her desk. As no files now remained on the left-hand side, the working day was over, and she leant back in her chair and rubbed her eyes. With characteristic good timing, Jane emerged through the adjoining door and placed a well-filled tumbler in front of Kate.

"All done?" she enquired.

"Yes."

Jane sat down in the single armchair opposite the large desk and both of the women sat silently, gulping down whisky.

"Any news on my car?" Kate asked.

"It's not going to be ready until tomorrow."

"Definitely tomorrow?"

"Yes, it'll be at your house, mid-morning. The service guy was very apologetic. Do you need it before then?"

"No, I'll be at home all weekend. Anyway, thanks for staying tonight. You must be famished?"

"Yes, starving."

Kate sighed. "Me too. I've nothing in the house, and I don't know that I can stand another restaurant."

Jane said, "How about popping over to my flat? I've a couple of steaks that won't last another day."

"Why not?"

Jane had already finished her drink, so Kate threw back the remainder in her own glass, then rose and picked up her coat from the stand at the side of the desk.

They poured themselves into the low bucket seats of Jane's sports car, and a short drive took them to her city-centre flat. After a short fumble in her handbag, Jane produced the key and they entered through the hall and into the main living room.

The room was large, spacious and eclectically furnished. A small glass table was surrounded by four capacious armchairs draped with unrelated covers. The armchairs looked out of place in the general environment, but when Kate had deposited her coat and collapsed within the nearest one, she discovered that at least they were comfortable.

Jane lifted Kate's coat. "I'll make a start."

Kate looked around the room. The walls were painted in a tasteful yet sorrowful pastel blue, adorned by a single picture. Kate wasn't interested in art but, in the way that all do when sitting insecurely in an unfamiliar place, rose to inspect it.

While Kate was deciding that the sea view with the two small girls playing at the edge of the water was not to her liking, Jane re-emerged and handed Kate another tumbler liberally filled with whisky.

"About ten minutes," Jane said.

"Can I give you a hand?" asked Kate wearily.

Jane laughed. "No, it's fine. Maybe you can set the table?"

A large pine table at the far end of the room was separated from the main area by three small steps. Kate looked around, and as no mats, plates nor cutlery were evident, she opened a drawer in the Welsh dresser which stood against the wall.

The Quartermaster

The drawer was untidy and home to an assortment of items: wrapping paper, string, tablecloths and, right at the rear, some placemats from several different sets. They would do the job, and Kate delved into the drawer. It was a mess and Kate had to remove most of the contents to get to them. As she did this, she disturbed a packet of photographs and several fell out.

She picked them up and skimmed a few: a selection of scenes from a summer wedding. The wedding was a fashionable affair with many guests in a large and expensive marquee. There was Jane. She was part of a small group of happy faces, which included the bride.

At that moment Jane emerged from the kitchen and looked over Kate's shoulder. Kate started. "Oh sorry, I didn't mean to be nosey."

Jane laughed. "My sister's wedding. I've got some more somewhere."

"Oh, no need. How's the food going?"

"Nearly there."

Kate followed Jane back to the kitchen. "Can I do anything?"

"No, it'll just be a few minutes. Have another drink."

Kate sat on one of the two stools and watched Jane at work. She was just as impressive at home as at work. Kate looked at her strong and handsome features, complemented by the perfect application of a little make-up and her luxuriant short brown hair.

Jane was saying something or other about wine but Kate wasn't listening. She was thinking about Jane. She realised that she knew very little about her. She had never heard Jane talk about men. Maybe Jane preferred women? She did not think so, and Kate thought she *would* know. Perhaps she had a lover back on the mainland?

"White or red?"

Kate recovered from her musings. "Oh, red please."

From the small wooden rack Jane produced a bottle and put it in front of Kate. "Is this all right?"

Of course it was all right. A 1968 burgundy, about £300 a bottle. Not bad on her salary.

A mobile phone rang. "Keep an eye on these steaks," Jane said, and ran off to retrieve her phone.

Kate wasn't trying to listen, but she could not help overhearing snatches of what seemed an animated conversation. Maybe this was the secret lover?

"No, it's not convenient right now,' Jane said firmly. 'I'll call you later." She returned to the kitchen and, without a word, resumed her duties, although Kate noted a faint flush had spread across her usually inscrutable features.

They talked little as they ate the meal, which was hardly surprising. Outside the workplace, what on earth would Kate, a middle-aged, working-class Ulsterwoman brought up on the Shankhill Road, have in common with a young, upper-class Englishwoman from London with her horses, fashionable parties and friends?

The meal was soon over and they relocated to the armchairs in the body of the room, sitting opposite each other. This was more relaxing, and when they had coffee, conversation became easier and more personal.

"What on earth made you come over to Belfast?" Kate asked.

"Why not?" replied Jane blandly.

"But surely with all your friends and everything in London . . . Besides, over there our image isn't the best."

"True enough," started Jane. "All my friends thought I was crazy, but I like to do my own thing." She looked at Kate. "Oh, you'll want to smoke. Go ahead, I don't mind. There's an ashtray there."

Kate rummaged in her handbag for the unopened packet that she knew to be there. "Damn, I thought I had a packet here."

"It's okay," Jane said. "There's a twenty-four-hour store just next door."

Kate made to rise, but before she could do so, Jane was at the door. "Sit down. I'll just be a minute."

When Jane had left, Kate looked at her watch. It was nearly eleven. She would need a taxi. Kate couldn't find her phone either, but that didn't matter because Jane's was sitting on the table.

Chapter 12

Jack was awake at seven, but today he didn't want to turn over and stay in bed. Beside him, Marion was asleep and did not stir as he got up. He leant across and kissed her lightly. It seemed that Mascar was suiting her, too.

As was now his firmly established daily custom, he edged slowly across the room and stood at the large bay window. It was the same view as the day before, and the day before that, but for Jack it was a daily reassurance that he was here.

The day that lay ahead was anticipated rather than dreaded. Especially today, because he had nothing to do. Well, nearly nothing. He would try to put off Amanda again and further defer reading up on the quarry project, concentrating instead on the visit of his eccentric accountant, Hamish Brown. He already liked Brown and walking had always been a pleasure to Jack, but he hadn't done much for years. Today was a good time to restart.

He drew away from the window and carefully crossed the room so as not to wake Marion. He slipped through the door, down the stairs and into the kitchen. Peering into the fridge, it was fuller than yesterday, but a further trip to Crawford's store was indicated. Jack, however, found that old habits die hard, and he bypassed the sausages, bacon, cheeses and fresh milk and selected a carton of grapefruit juice, which he carried over to the table. He swore as his attempt at opening the carton ended in a messy success. He poured a glass of the fruit juice and then, automatically, supplemented the juice with vodka from a bottle that had been carelessly left within his reach.

Vowing to put an end to this practice, he took a long mouthful of the mixture, lit a cigarette and drew deeply. When his coughing fit was over, he sat down to enjoy his breakfast. One drawback of rising early in Mascar was the dearth of reading material at that time. The daily newspapers arrived any time between midday and midnight, and there appeared to be little local dissatisfaction with this arrangement. Jack wasn't yet used to this. He looked around and spotted a pile of leaflets, which he pulled towards him. The first featured the Mascar Hotel and was unequivocal in its praise of the establishment. The leaflet boasted of freshly prepared local produce, specialist sea foods and unrivalled panoramic delights, all naturally allied to a meaningless and bland promise of a warm and friendly atmosphere. Jack doubted the veracity of these and the numerous other claims that seemed at odds with his own impression of the place, but what else could a publicity brochure say?

He opened the leaflet out. The centre spread was dominated by a photograph of McAllister and a woman, no doubt Mrs McAllister. McAllister looked hearty and welcoming with a beaming red face, whereas his wife looked unhappy. Mrs McAllister was a small, thin and careworn woman of about fifty. Her hair was grey, and although she beamed a smile at the reader, a second glance exposed it as being thinner and more forced than that of her husband.

"Morag and Jim McAllister extend a warm welcome," the caption read. Jack tossed it aside and selected the next from the pile.

This leaflet was a single-sheet flyer printed on coarse, cheap paper and detailed the Free Church's weekly timetable of worship and other activities. It was many years since Jack had attended church and his most recent visits had been confined to weddings and funerals. It wasn't that he had no religion – indeed, no man so vulnerable and insecure as him could afford to be without it – but simply that his beliefs had evolved in irregular phases. Now, so abstract did they seem when assembled, they could no longer sit comfortably within any established religion.

He would probably have to make concessions. The Free Church of Scotland, although not as powerful as in former times, still exerted considerable influence within the local community on both religious and secular issues. It was inconceivable that he would not come into contact with it soon.

How soon, even Jack had not anticipated.

Chapter 13

The Reverend Thomas McCallum was a tall man, yet he stooped as if laid low by the sins of his flock. There had been many changes in his parish over the six decades of McCallum's life. He was a native of Mascar and save for half a dozen years at the University of Glasgow, he had never lived anywhere else. On leaving Mascar he had been determined to return; however, he had hoped to experience more of life outside when the sudden death of his predecessor, all those years ago, had given him a chance to return that he could not pass up.

God's work was just as vital in a remote area such as Mascar as it was in a modern sprawling city. In many ways it was *more* vital. Problems in Mascar were no less severe, but support agencies were absent and McCallum filled in for all of them.

And then there were the newcomers. Although McCallum had frequently lectured the locals on the economic gains afforded to the area by the rash of new settlers, he was far from convinced. They were often overbearing and arrogant, and, worst of all, he despised their secular or Romanist ways.

McCallum was breathing heavily now. The cliff road, which he used to run up as a boy, was now getting its own back. He steeled himself for the final push and, with difficulty, attained the high point of the road. The wind was freshening and he would have preferred to be indoors, but today he had a vital duty to perform: to personally welcome every newcomer to the village, whether they wanted welcoming or not.

In respect of the latest potential addition to his flock, McCallum was fighting a losing battle in his attempt to keep an open mind. From what he knew and had heard of Jack Edwards, McCallum feared he would fit exactly to the template of the advanced village gossip.

McCallum was also uneasy about the quarry. It had taken him the best part of two years to prevail upon Miss Edwards to stop Sunday working. She had been sympathetic but had received robust advice from the professionals on the necessity of seven-day working. In addition, a number of locals were resentful; they saw McCallum's fight as one that would lose them lucrative overtime payments. In spite of this, McCallum had prevailed. She had been a good woman, Miss Edwards.

He entered the drive to the large house and doubted whether Miss Edwards' nephew would prove so staunch an ally.

He took a long, deep breath, straightened himself and heard the peal of the bell as he pressed the button twice. The man whom McCallum regarded was an unimpressive sight, roughly dressed in an ill-fitting pair of trousers and a checked tartan shirt with only a few of the buttons fastened. Barely fit for gardening. The man was middle-aged and sported longish, unkempt hair. It appeared to McCallum that he had been up all-night drinking.

It wasn't a great start.

Chapter 14

Jack cursed, stubbed out a cigarette and buttoned up his shirt. Visitors at this time were as unwelcome as they were unexpected. Maybe Hamish had come early?

Many religious representatives exuded an air of understanding benevolence, but the man standing in front of Jack and filling most of the doorway did not. He was tall, about sixty and stood staring ahead, his craggy fixed features the embodiment of Protestant defiance.

"Good morning, minister, what can I do for you?"

Thomas McCallum, the Free Presbyterian minister of the parish, introduced himself in breathless tones.

After a handshake, a short difficult pause ensued before Jack belatedly concluded that McCallum had not struggled up the cliff road simply to shake hands. "Er, sorry, please come in."

He led the way into the hall and stopped abruptly. Where to? Nearly all of the rooms were unprepared for visitors. The kitchen, with its overflowing ashtray and vodka bottle, seemed all wrong somehow.

Dithering now and feeling increasingly awkward, Jack led McCallum into the small den. "Come in here. Sorry, but we're not really organised. We've just been here a couple of days."

McCallum cast a wintery glance at Jack, and then, after a suspicious appraisal, accepted a seat on one of the two armchairs beside the unlit open fire.

Again, an uneasy silence descended until McCallum said, "I think we have met before, Mr Edwards."

"Yes probably, I spent quite a few summers here when I was a boy."

"And are you planning to make this your permanent home?"

McCallum was certainly nosey. "Yes, I think so," Jack said calmly.

"There's a lot to do. A lot of responsibility," McCallum said ominously.

"Yes," Jack admitted. "I'm afraid that my aunt rather lost her grip on things near the end."

"She was a fine woman, your aunt." Then, as if to alert Jack to the criteria by which he too would be judged, he added "She was very generous to the villagers and, of course, a great supporter of the church and its works. In an area like Mascar, the church and its members play a crucial role. There are many problems, you know."

Jack did know. His current and overriding problem was how to get rid of McCallum. He resented the intrusion, unannounced, at this time of the morning, and although he had nodded in sympathetic agreement, Jack didn't really understand. Maybe he would in time. Right now, Mascar was a place of joy to him, a new start. That it, too, was touched with commonplace and grubby everyday difficulties he refused to allow right now.

The minister wasn't finished. "At the moment we are engaged in a community campaign to raise money for a small extension to the village hall." He paused, allowing Jack the opportunity to spring in and demonstrate his own enthusiasm as well as, no doubt, his sponsorship of the project.

Jack partially obliged. "Of course, I'd be very happy to help in any way that I can." Although this stopped short of the ringing endorsement McCallum might have hoped for, he did not show it and, indeed, his expression lightened a little as he thanked Jack, expressing affected surprise at this unsolicited offer.

If Jack, however, had hope that this wintery smile marked a thawing in relations, he was wrong. McCallum breathed in loudly, raised his head and cleared his throat in a portentous fashion, a sure presage of a difficult moment to follow. And so it proved.

"I would like to ask, Mr Edwards, if you intend to reopen the quarry?"

Up until this point Jack had felt disadvantaged by the sudden appearance of the man of God; however, his resolve hardened on receipt of this question. He replied, equally pompously, "I'm afraid I've had very little time to consider the matter."

As a conversation stopper, this did not work. "I quite understand that these are early days," the minister replied, "but I must tell you that while the church council are not opposed, in principle, to any redevelopment, we have a number of concerns."

Jack bit his lip and sat back in his chair.

"When the quarry was open it brought many outsiders into the area, and, with them, crime and drunkenness. There were heavy lorries on the road at all times, day and night, and" – McCallum summoned all of his gravitas – "there was, for many years, work carried out on the Sabbath."

Jack wasn't surprised at the line – a Free Church of Scotland minister was likely to take it after all – but McCallum might have had the manners to wait until asked. Up until now he had been searching for ways of resisting what had seemed an irresistible tide running in favour of the redevelopment.

But not anymore. He was damned if he would strike up an alliance with McCallum. His sureness and certainty could maybe be suffered, but not in Jack's home.

He didn't want a row, but he had self-respect. He said stiffly, "I must say, Mr McCallum, that while I'm sure you have a genuine interest in the matter, I rather resent being hectored on this matter, especially when I've only just arrived and can hardly be expected to have formed a final conclusion. Of course," he added, concerned that he might have gone a little far, "all sorts of views will have to be considered before I finally decide, and I would certainly wish to have the views of yourself and the church authorities."

Jack's expression was firm and he had looked directly at McCallum when delivering this statement.

This resolution apparently worked. McCallum, quite suddenly, said, "Yes, thank you. We will look forward to these consultations.' He struggled out of his seat.

With the meeting over, Jack relaxed and enjoyed escorting McCallum to the front door. When McCallum turned to again shake hands, both were distracted by the sounds of footsteps on the staircase.

Amanda, yawning and fixing her morning hair, was wearing a loose-fitting shirt that was struggling to conceal her form. As she descended, each step revealed a lot of her legs and one or two glimpses of her high-cut briefs.

Without a word, McCallum scowled, turned on his heel and left, which provided an appropriate final scene to an unsatisfactory meeting.

Chapter 15

As Jack watched McCallum embark on his slow descent down the cliff path, the minister was passed by a battered old estate car beating an irregular path up the hill. From the model of car and the alarmingly fast and careless driving, Jack felt sure that it would be Brown. A moment later the car was parked in the drive and Brown and two lively dogs emerged. Brown was kitted in rough and worn tweeds with a matching hat and a cigarette smouldering in his mouth.

"Morning, morning!" he exclaimed heartily as he thrust out his hand. "I see you've had the pleasure of meeting the Reverend McCallum."

"Yes." Jack nodded, still looking after the solitary figure descending the cliff road. "I'm afraid I may have been a bit rude to him."

"Oh, never mind that," said Brown. "It's easy to do. The man would try the patience of a saint." Brown's dogs were fussing around Jack and he was nervously countering them when Brown noticed his discomfort. "I see you don't like dogs," he correctly deduced.

"No, well, I was always a little wary of them," Jack admitted.

Brown issued a couple of snappy commands to the beasts and they momentarily retreated. "Yes, I agree, they're bloody pests. A legacy from the ex-wife, I'm afraid. In fact, all I was left with," he added dolefully and aimed an affectionate kick at the dogs.

The dogs were utterly different, the larger one about the size of a sheepdog, yet with an unsettlingly large head rather like that of a German Shepherd. Its features and markings were surely original and the beast was the result, Jack thought, of God knows what type of union. It was, at least, less active than its smaller companion, a hyperactive type of terrier that seemed to enjoy baring its teeth at all comers. It was possible that the pair might be useful for something, but he could see no utility or merit in either of them.

"Come in," Jack said, and men and dogs made their way through the door and into the kitchen.

Marion was out of bed now and she and Amanda were seated at the table, eating breakfast. Amanda was still wearing her shirt and looked about as sexy as it was possible to look at this time of the morning. Marion was wearing a pair of pyjamas and she looked just as good.

Neither of them seemed fazed by the arrival of Brown and his dogs, and Jack introduced everyone.

"Have you eaten?" Marion asked.

"No," Brown said, "I'm starving."

"Help yourself, there's some bacon and toast over there."

Brown helped himself and sat down. "We're going to climb the two hills at the back of the house today. It's just a hop. It'll take no more than three or four hours. It's great exercise and the views from the top are spectacular. Why don't you join us?"

"Not me. I've got some work to do – on a book." Amanda looked at Jack and he smiled back sheepishly.

"Nor me," Marion said. "I've a lot of work to do here."

Jack felt a bit guilty now, and he looked at Marion.

"Oh no, you go. I need peace and quiet. Besides, you look like you need exercise."

Everyone else smiled in agreement except Jack, although he knew this was fair comment.

"Give me ten minutes and I'll be ready."

Chapter 16

At about midday Jane decided that she had slept long enough. She made her way to the bathroom and sleepwalked into the shower. The hot water did the trick, and within minutes she was planning what to do with her day.

This planning was more concerned with the detail rather than the activity. She would climb. She rarely did anything else at weekends and it gave her great pleasure to engage in this solitary pursuit. She had no real friends over here; she'd had enough of that scene in London. Fresh air, exercise and peace and quiet were what she liked.

She finished showering and hastily assembled her kit, which seemed to be in order, and within ten minutes was in her car and speeding towards the north coast of County Antrim.

The roads were quiet and she made good progress. After a drive of some fifty miles she turned off the main road and proceeded down a narrow coastal track. The day was fine and dry and the wind light, perfect for climbing. She stopped the car in a small circular parking area at the end of the track, walked down to a rough beach and stared up at the cliffs, looking up for a suitable route.

The Quartermaster

At first sight the cliffs seemed sheer, but she was experienced and was soon confident that she had identified a possible route well within her capabilities. She tested the rock. It was dry and strong with plentiful holds. She appraised the route for a few more minutes and decided to go.

She estimated the cliff-face at about 300 feet high: a climb of about an hour. She was in no hurry, however, and she felt the thrill that she always felt when, having secured her initial hold, she moved onto the face.

The climb was largely straightforward with deep and secure holds plentiful; however, as she neared the final pitch, it unexpectedly got trickier than anticipated. The overhang was now pronounced and the rock was smoother and, worse, water from a minor waterfall cascaded through the only suitable approach section. Just before this section there was a good-sized abutting ledge and this, at least, would allow her to stop, sit and restore her strength.

She pulled herself onto the ledge. It was flat and wide and she sat comfortably, looking out to sea and steeling herself for the final section. She looked down. It was getting dark and colder now in the short winter days. In the dark the descent would be impossible, and worse, out to sea, the sky was darkening and what looked like heavy black rain clouds were moving quickly her way – ten minutes if she was lucky.

This discouraging analysis concluded, she breathed in deeply and considered her first move. It was risky. A climber should never lose all contact with the rock, yet her only prospect was to leap round and over the overhang and trust that she could gain some type of handhold on the top. This meant springing powerfully up and out and just bypassing the extreme edge of the boulder.

She crouched and rocked up and down on the balls of her feet several times. Her calf muscles loosened, she took a last deep breath and then sprang into the air.

Time seemed elastic as her body feathered but successfully bypassed the edge of the outcrop and her outstretched arms landed hard on the top of the rock. A moment later her face crashed on to the rock and, for a split second, she was in perfect equilibrium – neither rising nor falling – and then, slowly at first and then more quickly, she began to slide backwards.

Backwards off the boulder towards the beach below. Backwards to her death. She was sliding slowly and there was a chance, although not a great one, that her hands would be able to get purchase on the black boulder. She shaped her hands as claws. The skin from her fingertips was shredding and blood poured freely from her mouth, but there wasn't time to think about that.

Then it happened. Only inches from the edge of the boulder, her right hand felt a depression in the otherwise smooth rock. She gripped furiously, gripped the rock for her life. Her right hand stuck but it wasn't going to hold her for long. She was sliding back again. Still her left hand could gain no purchase. The hold on her right hand was strong but the jerk, when it came, would require all of her strength, and it probably wouldn't be enough.

The jerk came. She felt the strain from her toes to her fingernails and two of her secure right-hand fingers came loose. There was no time to consider her next move. There was only one option now. Only one chance. All on this one shot. She restored her two fingers to her right-hand grip and, straining her abdomen and summoning all her power, she heaved. She rose quickly at first. Her chin came level with the top of the rock, but her arm was shaking and the pain was barely endurable. Before she could locate a suitable grip for her left hand, the top of the rock and her right hand again began fading out of view.

Living was worth a final effort and, with contorted face and a deafening bellow, she lifted herself on top of the flat rock, where she lay prone and exhausted.

Then she must have passed out, for when she woke the rain was coming down hard. But it didn't matter now. The sharp, cool impact of the rain on her face told her she was alive. Through the gloom she estimated that no more than ten feet of the cliff remained and, by comparison with the last section, there would be no difficulties. She would be able to walk up. She slowly lifted herself. Everything hurt, but she was elated and, after a few minutes, she emerged onto the grassy top of the cliff at a small viewpoint and car park.

But even this short scramble exhausted her, and she collapsed to the ground, lying flat and face down on the grass, breathing hard. Suddenly she broke into lung-bursting laughter. She was safe.

She lifted her head up and, still lying on the wet grass, rested it in her hands and looked forward towards the car park. There was one car in the car park, and as she watched, she saw the door open and a tall figure emerge. It was very dark now and it was impossible to distinguish the features of the form slowly walking towards her.

The figure neared. It looked like a woman. After a few more steps, there was no doubt. It was a familiar gait. "Kate? Kate! Is that you?"

No reply came back and the figure continued its silent advance until it halted and knelt down in front of her. Kate looked her over quickly and exclaimed, "My God, Jane! Are you all right?"

Jane laughed with relief. "Yes, I think so."

She made to stand up and removed her hands from her face for the attempt. She lost Kate's eyes for a moment and, when she regained them, the gun butt was moving on its unwavering course. As her head turned, it caught her flush on the temple and Jane went spinning backwards, rapidly descending 300 feet to the bottom of the cliff.

Chapter 17

After walking only a few hundred feet up a moderate gradient, Jack had insisted on a stop on the pretext of being able, for the first time, to take a proper view of the house and its setting. It was certainly true that the spot chosen was admirably suited to the purpose but, in truth, Jack had shot his bolt in the attempt to keep up with Hamish's early pace and was experiencing a well-earned range of symptoms reserved for the wretchedly unconditioned. For a man who could out-smoke and out-drink Jack (a feat which took some doing) and give away about ten years, Hamish was in incredible shape.

They sat leaning against a well-placed boulder, and for a few minutes Jack struggled to talk. He was trying to breathe, trying to get down to the bottom of his lungs and fill them with refreshing oxygen, but he couldn't.

Hamish was sympathetic. "Aye, takes a wee while to get used to this again. Take your time."

"I will," Jack spluttered. He looked down at the house. Its prominence, both in location and size, was even more apparent from this vantage point. It towered over the village and, to the observer, it was immediately obvious that someone of local importance lived there. Jack rather liked that. The full extent of the grounds was also well-defined. A low drystane boundary wall meandered irregularly around the house, and enclosed a number of irregularly placed outbuildings. There was a large double garage on the west side, with several sheds of varying sizes.

Hamish drew on a cigarette. "It's a grand spot."

Jack nodded in agreement. "How long have you lived here?"

Hamish gazed out to the horizon, drew on his cigarette and said, "Oh, I was born in this area. Just in the next village, in fact. I lived here until I went to university. I met my wife there." He paused as if recalling a sad and regrettable episode in his life. "I wanted to come back, but she wouldn't hear of it, so I was stuck in the city for nearly twenty years. God knows how I stood it."

Bitterness replaced regret in his voice now. "Rotary Clubs, golf clubs. Working furiously to stand still in the material stakes. I didn't realise just how much I hated it until I came back."

Jack had known Hamish for only a couple of days, but already he felt they were close. "And, do you know, she left me, bloody left me, for some pot-bellied sixty-year-old businessman."

"Children?" Jack asked.

"No. Always wanted them myself but, of course, we both had to have our careers. They were always part of the plan, though. Suppose it's as well. I'd never have got away then." He stopped again, as if about to comment further. But he finally settled on, "Shall we press on?"

Jack rose wearily. The dogs were ready and they bounded quickly over the easy going of the firm uplands. The breeze was slight and the skies clearing as they ascended. Jack, having recovered his wind, required no further rest breaks, and they did not stop again until they both stood on the small, rocky summit of the first of the two peaks.

They sat in silence for a long time, taking in the scene, and eating the crude sandwiches Jack had earlier prepared. "Do you have many dealings with Sutherland?" Jack asked.

"Yes, quite a few. In a small place like this one can hardly avoid contact with one's fellow professionals."

"How do you like him?" Showing his own hand to encourage mutual frankness, Jack added, "He wasn't my cup of tea."

"Oh, he's all right," Hamish said. "Just a bit too intense. I think he actually believes that his work is important." Brown shook his head at this thought and muttered, "Mad, mad." He outstretched his arms to indicate the sea and the hills on view from the peak. "That's what's important."

He was right about that.

Hamish shook his head and added a final criticism, "And, of course, he doesn't drink!"

Hamish had had a narrow escape. He had been living out a life without purpose and without pleasure, but he had escaped. Jack, too, had escaped.

After the rigours of ascending the first peak, the walk to the second was plain sailing. There was only a small drop in height, and the natural path didn't deviate from the ridge, which made the route continually interesting. The breeze was now rising with the altitude, and it carried a chill edge as it struck Jack's face. They did not linger so long on the second peak, and before long were engaged in a slightly hazardous descent off the side of the peak and down to a beach a little way from the village.

The tide was far out, and its retreat had exposed miles of fine, smooth sand. It was a beach to rival any, and for once Jack found himself glad of prevailing weather conditions in the north-west. But for this paradoxical blessing of inclement weather, Mascar would be a holiday paradise for the masses. There would be a pier, amusement centres, caravan parks and other horrors. He looked around. There were none of these monstrosities. It was all his, and he gave an involuntary skip of joy. The dogs were happy, too, meeting and leaving Hamish with long sweeps which took them to the water's edge and back.

From beach level, Jack could not see up to the house, although he could see the white outline of the hotel visible in the distance. It was continually in his line of sight as they walked and, as he looked ahead, he saw a Jaguar speed along the village road, and then it was out of sight. It looked like Amanda's car.

After some twenty minutes more idling on the beach, they neared the village. The sand gave way to slippery brown rocks, but they negotiated them easily enough and quickly were over the sea wall and into the public bar.

Inside, things were very like yesterday. McAllister sat with the McRae brothers at a large table which was crowded with empty glasses – evidence of a session that had been long and was far from over.

McAllister looked up and returned to the bar.

"Two malts, doubles, and two pints of Guinness," Hamish said.

"You going to join us?"

Hamish accepted this offer to buy three more drinks and they sat down with the others.

"We've been walking," Hamish said.

There was no reply, and as Jack looked it seemed to him that the superficial expressions of welcome had marginally, but perceptibly, dissipated. Jack began to suspect that their arrival had caused the premature demise of an earlier and more interesting conversation.

The Quartermaster

He had not formally met the McRae brothers, and when the silence continued, Jack corrected this by introducing himself and offering his hand to the nearest brother.

The brothers were both about forty. The nearest one had a narrow face with a full head of lank, black hair tied at the back in a ponytail. He had wispy hair on both his chin and his upper lip, which looked as if they would like to meet but both were too shy to make the first move. His face was battered and rough and told of a lifetime engaged in manual work in an unyielding environment. This turned out to be Tom, and he met Jack's hand with a firm handshake and a low grunt. This done, he did not feel the need for further comment and returned his attention to the glass of whisky in front of him.

His sibling, by contrast, had no worries about hair management. His head was round, bald and shiny, and it was, Jack noticed, continually on his mind if his right hand, which constantly, unconsciously and unsuccessfully moved to cover the fact, was any guide. His expression was more relaxed than that of his brother, although hardly jovial. Ian McRae, like his brother, wore an ill-fitting pair of denims, stout working boots and a heavy, ribbed jumper.

He was more loquacious. "Pleased to meet you, Mr Edwards."

"This is Hamish, Hamish Brown," Jack said.

"Aye, we know Hamish," Ian McRae said.

Remembering McAllister's advice of the previous day, Jack said, "I've a couple of sheds with rotten roofs. And there's the scaffolding round the house. Some re-pointing I understand. Can you help me out?"

The brothers looked at each other in silent conference. Eventually, Tom, who was evidently the brains of the operation, furrowed his forehead as if juggling a huge number of prior commitments. After a pause he ventured, "Aye, we could have a look tomorrow."

"What time?"

This proved a more difficult question, and Jack settled for a promise of "sometime in the afternoon". With this, the brothers, in perfect synchronicity, lifted their glasses, drained them, rose and left.

When they left, McAllister observed, "It's not easy to pin these boys down."

"Will they show up tomorrow?"

McAllister had no doubts. "Oh yes, they don't say much, but if they do, they'll keep to it. They'll see you tomorrow all right."

Hamish's glass was already empty and he toyed with it in body language that could not be misinterpreted. McAllister obliged and again rose and refilled the drinks. Once again, he did not ask for money. Normally Jack would have been delighted with such an arrangement, but as he owned a part of the hotel, he dipped into his pocket and proffered a twenty-pound note to McAllister, who pushed it back, laughing.

It was easy to be generous with other people's money.

Chapter 18

Kate Phillips poured herself a large glass of supermarket red wine and sat back on her sofa.

She always knew this day would come, and she was ready for it. She had had a good run, and whatever happened she was determined to quit on a high. The deal had taken a long time, but it would serve her organisation for years. A few weeks and it would be dispersed and hidden in dumps all over the country. She was nearly there.

She lit a cigarette. Her cover had been deep and rock solid for years, but that looked blown now. Had she become complacent? And what of her mistakes?

In the modern world, all manner of ultra-sophisticated surveillance techniques were available to security services, but Kate was thinking more about the oldest and most traditional strategy; in particular, whether Peter had been the only spy in her organisation.

He would have been an easy recruit. A loudmouth that spent money freely, with a flexible set of beliefs, none more important than those favouring himself. She had made a mistake there. Even when she received news of him meeting Jane, she had, at first, assumed it was just about sex – with Peter as the predator. Routinely, she had dug a bit deeper and established that the men that Jane had "accidentally" encountered on her climbing days were mostly known to Kate.

Kate had liked Jane and she didn't really want to kill her, but she had had no choice. Jane had made a bad mistake, and mistakes were usually deadly in this business. And she had had some bad luck: the photograph in Jane's flat when she had innocently pointed out her father. A proud father at a wedding. Colonel Pierce of British Intelligence. One of the most senior operatives in the intelligence services. Kate had seen that face many times in the dossiers she herself used for her briefings.

She refilled her glass and shook her head. Maybe it was as well she was going to have to quit. It was amazing that she had not been suspicious of Jane. What the fuck was a woman like Jane doing in Belfast if not working for British Intelligence?

If the penetration was confined to Peter, things were not all lost. Peter knew about the arms purchase, and he had some dealings with Littlejohn, but that had been only as a courier paying money to one of Littlejohn's middlemen.

She would probably soon find out. Both Peter and Jane were dead. Even without direct evidence, the deaths of both in quick succession would hardly be treated as coincidental, and if British Intelligence were out of spies they would need to improvise – and quickly. They would suspect her of using the bank, but Jane hadn't known anything about that. Kate was sure of that.

Internal controls within the bank, especially for someone in her lofty position, were as inadequate as in the next place, and her arrangements were complex and labyrinthine. But nothing was undetectable.

Kate wasn't certain how long she could keep such investigations at bay, so the accounts had to be moved. Not, however, in a sudden and irregular fashion, but with a series of modest movements using backdated authorities.

Kate turned the music up loud and began singing tunelessly in accompaniment. She had another difficulty. She needed a new secretary.

Chapter 19

It was dark and a few drinks later when Jack and Hamish emerged from the hotel bar. It was colder than before and the wind had freshened. As they turned to take the road up to the house, Jack searched in his pockets and discovered that he had only a few cigarettes left.

He turned to go back to the hotel but, noticing that the light was still on in Miss Crawford's shop, changed his mind. McAllister's kept some cigarettes but not his brand. As he walked along the road and into the shop, he passed a large parked car. The familiar bells rang out as he entered but, unlike yesterday, he was not attended immediately. From the back of the shop he could hear raised voices, a man's and a woman's. Surely they must have heard the bell? Maybe not: they were talking loud enough to wake the dead.

Despite this, he could not make out the details of the conversation, and he decided to stop trying to. He moved back from the counter to the door and, reaching up, gave the bells a vigorous ring. This did the trick and the voices from the back room first lowered, then ceased, and a few seconds later Crawford emerged.

"Oh, hello," she said carelessly, avoiding his gaze.
"Can I have forty Marlboro, please?" he said.

She turned to the shelf behind her and he noticed that she looked different. Although the blouse and mid-length skirt were hardly adventurous, it was as though she had made, for her, a big effort.

She handed him the cigarettes without a word and he paid. She handed him his change, again without speaking or catching his eye, and Jack, who had wanted to ask her for some information on shopping issues, decided it had already been difficult enough for her, mumbled a few words and left the shop. As he did, he heard the sound of the door being locked behind him.

He re-joined Hamish in the street and had a good look at the opulent saloon car. "Whose car's that?"

"No idea."

After a stiff walk up the hill to the house, made more difficult by the now biting wind and the amount of alcohol they had consumed, they arrived at the house. Jack noted that Amanda's car was absent, although the house was ablaze with light. The front door was unlocked. He went through to the kitchen, but although he could smell food cooking, Marion wasn't there. He returned to Hamish in the hall and, hearing Marion calling from the study, made his way there.

The study was in darkness, save for the light of a powerful desk lamp. He walked towards her and she looked up, pushing her spectacles from her eyes. She rose from the seat and embraced him affectionately in the middle of the room.

"What you doing?" Jack asked.

She smiled. "Looking over some of the papers you missed yesterday."

"Yes, well, I'd have got round to them."

"We've got to get a grip on our affairs."

He didn't mind the rebuke and was thrilled at her use of the word "our". He had never heard her use the word so freely and naturally. He moved to her and for a moment held her tight.

"You hungry?" she asked after a moment.

"Yes, that's the most exercise I've done in years. I've got Hamish outside."

"There's a stew in the oven. It'll be ready in a few minutes. I'll join you in a moment."

Jack returned to Hamish, led him into the den and poured drinks. "There's some food ready. You'll stay, of course. Stay over if you want?"

"No, I can't. I must get back tonight."

"You sure? We've had a few drinks."

Brown was in no doubt. "I'm fine. If I fall asleep the dogs will wake me."

Marion shouted, "Food's ready."

Hamish downed his drink. "Okay, I'm off. I'll give you a ring. Maybe get out again soon?"

Jack saw Hamish out and went into the kitchen. "Where's Amanda?"

"She's gone back to London. There was a phone call. She was a bit upset; I think. She said to tell you that she would be back mid-week. I think there's something wrong with her father."

Chapter 20

At five o'clock on Monday morning, Kate Phillips was up, dressed and drinking a strong black coffee at her kitchen table. It was going to be a big day.

Over the weekend, she firmed her previous conviction that early action on her part was essential. They would come soon, she was sure. Any interruption to their flow of information would be disastrous. Delays would cool, maybe kill, the trail. They couldn't wait.

It would take weeks to complete the purpose-built units that would provide permanent homes for the weapons. They were safe for the moment – safe for a number of months – but they were too far away. They could be needed here at any time, close at hand. Every day the uneasy peace creaked and groaned. The war was coming.

At this time the roads would be deserted, but driving wasn't an option today, and a ten-minute walk in the bitter cold took her to the rarely used back entrance to the bank. She let herself into her office unobserved and locked the door behind her. She threw her coat carelessly over the stand and, before sitting, looked through to the adjacent office that had been Jane's. A light sensation of Jane's perfume still lingered in the tidy room. One of her work maxims had always been to clear all loose administrative ends by the end of the working week in case, she used to say, "One was run over by a bus." How prescient and sensible such an approach was. One, indeed, never did know.

Kate made her own coffee and began to tap her keyboard. Like all good frauds, hers was a very simple one. International hot money regularly came and went through banks. These large, short-term deposits were arranged on a case-by-case basis, by her personally. It was a simple matter for Kate to agree such terms with the client, pass the money through an intermediate account and then to the bank's own credit with the official charges programmed in – a fraction of a decimal point lower than that agreed – with the overflow collecting in her own accounts. The speed at which the terms had to be agreed along with the lack of paperwork, the transitory nature of the deposits made and the shadiness of some of the depositors were all factors in her favour. Hundreds of these transactions occurred annually, but she employed the approach carefully and selectively. In this way she had, over several years, built up a fund of many millions of pounds for her organisation. It was so easy for her. None of her directors, and certainly none of her so-called risk managers, knew more about the trading systems. It had taken her years.

She checked all the accounts carefully. Nothing was wrong. A few had high credit balances; she would flatten them out. Larger-sized accounts would be examined first. She rose and made her way through to the adjoining office and examined the files stored on the personal computer. After a little trial and error, she had printed out the relevant forms and started the paperwork. By six she was finished. She hurriedly threw on her coat and walked briskly out of the rear door of the building unseen.

Half an hour later, she arrived back at the bank and parked in her usual space, being careful to engage the night security guard in conversation. It wasn't long after that that her phone buzzed, and a few minutes later two men and a woman stood in front of Kate's desk.

A tall, good-humoured, handsome suit opened the discussion, "Good morning, Miss Phillips. I'm Gerald Halton, Head Office Support Unit." He indicated the others and introduced them as Anne Patrick and Frank Barras.

"An unscheduled inspection?" Kate asked.

Gerald Halton sounded bored. "Yes, sorry. Should be a couple of days at the most. When was your last inspection?"

"Only nine months ago."

"Oh, well, as you know these timings are just random."

These platitudes were uninteresting, and Kate wasn't really listening to them. The cover was quite reasonable, although she didn't believe a word of it.

Maybe Halton or Anne Patrick did, but not, she thought, the other man, the short, stout middle-aged man who stood furthest back. Frank Barras looked out of place in the company of these young thrusters – he was fifty, maybe sixty, sartorially deficient, and he wore an expression that told of a man passed over for promotion so many times he no longer cared. Like Kate, he wasn't listening to his young leader.

"When could we get started?" Halton asked.

Kate considered. "Well, if you could wait until my secretary comes in, she will be able to look after you. She's usually in by eight thirty."

"Yes fine, thank you, Miss Phillips."

"Let me get you some drinks. Tea, coffee?"

With this, they all sat down. More small talk, but Kate and the little fat man with the blue grey eyes knew that, whatever else, Kate's secretary wouldn't be in today.

Chapter 21

Amanda stood sinking into the deep pile of the carpet of the high-ceilinged and elegantly appointed room. The man behind the desk was speaking, flanked by two others. His words were delivered by a clear, firm and deep voice that filled the cavernous room. Amanda listened in silence, staring straight ahead. She was a professional and a tough modern woman, and the tears that cascaded down her cheeks proved it.

The man behind the desk was about sixty with a full head of black hair which, although carelessly managed, achieved a striking effect. His jaw was strong and his piercing blue eyes completed a perfect picture. His suit was of a standard cut, but his tall, broad frame wore it well. He was the only man she absolutely trusted, and the only one she obeyed unquestioningly.

Amanda's father continued, "She was on an assignment. A dangerous assignment, but we think it was probably an accident. She took needless risks."

"Probably?"

"We just don't know yet. She was on an active assignment."

He moved from behind his desk, joined her in the centre of the room and enveloped her in his arms. He held her very tight because she was all he had left in the whole world now.

They held this position for a long time then suddenly broke off.

"Okay, tell me about this assignment."

Her father told her.

"So, do nothing at the moment?" Amanda asked.

"Nothing. Wait until you hear from me, but stand by."

She kissed him on the cheek, hugged him again and turned and left the room. Walking down a few corridors, she ignored the eyes of the clerks who, with inadequate discretion, stared at her as she passed. With her head high and her gaze fixed ahead, she emerged onto the busy London street.

She walked blindly along the pavement. The crowds of people and the noise of the traffic were invisible and inaudible. When you lost someone you loved, your best friend, it felt like nothing else in the world. She became irrationally angry with the crowds on the busy street. Off to work or to shop or meet friends. What problems did *they* have? After walking for a while, her contempt and loathing for the human race subsided and she bought some newspapers and went into a café. To the exasperation of the proprietor she hung around there for a long time, buying only a coffee and several refills. Somehow this worked a bit, and after an hour or so she was ready to go home.

Her flat was cold, and the door opened with difficulty against the force of an unattractive pile of mail lying on the floor. She gathered up the collection of envelopes and made her way through to the lounge. Without removing her coat, she sat at a dining table and began disinterestedly to open them. None were important, and she stood up and walked across the room to the flashing light of her telephone. The messages weren't very interesting either. Until the last one.

The woman's voice was instantly familiar. Amanda moved close to the telephone and listened intently. She played the message again. She sat quite still, a single tear sliding down her cheek. It was now mid-afternoon. She made a decision.

She picked up the telephone, and on discovering that she could make the last flight, booked a ticket to Glasgow.

She telephoned again. "Hi Marion, it's Amanda."

"Hi you. Is everything okay?"

"Oh, just some urgent business. Look I've booked a plane, and I can get to you late tonight, if that's okay with you?"

"Yes, of course. Why wouldn't it be?"

"Well, I just was wondering if I was getting in the way. I mean, you've just moved in."

"Don't be silly. You sure you're okay?"

"Well, I've been better to be honest."

Marion said, "Hmm. Get up here and we can have a chat. When are you due in?"

"Nine or ten, all being well."

"Okay, I'll stay up, but if I fall asleep, the front door will be open. We can do that in Mascar."

"Thanks, I appreciate that. See you soon."

Amanda felt a bit better now. Marion always said, and usually did, the right thing. They were so different in many ways, but they had been close since their university days.

Her taxi was here. She made for the door but, before leaving, she turned, walked over to the telephone and erased all the messages.

Chapter 22

Jack was washing dishes and being useful when Marion sidled up to him.

"What did you learn from the files, then?" he asked.

"Well, things seem in good order. Sutherland seems to be efficient enough, generally."

"Generally?"

"Oh, I've got a few queries, but I'm sure we can clear them up soon."

"What about that damn quarry?"

Marion put her arm round him and squeezed him a bit. "I think we should open it, Jack. It'll create so many jobs around here, and from what I can see, they're desperately needed. But …"

"But what?"

"I don't think we should give it to either the Thompson Group or the Peters Consortium."

"But they're the only two firms that have made a bid."

"No. There's Murray."

"Murray?"

"Oh," she said, "I know Thompson and Peters are well-established, large firms and their plans and documents were polished and well researched, but why do we need to have anonymous multinational companies on our land? Why not go with a local bid?"

"Murray …" Jack mused. "I think I saw something on it. Wasn't there a report saying that Murray was too small and lacked the expertise to be taken seriously?"

"Well, it's true that that report said so, but I don't know. I didn't think the objections were insurmountable, and besides, if they needed to expand to take on the project, so much the better."

"Sounds risky to me. Quarrying's a specialist operation. If we're to reopen we'd have to be sure that it wasn't being operated by cowboys, local or otherwise. If we want to consider Murray, we'd have to be pretty sure that they can do the job." He added warily, "All the advisers, and probably even they themselves, think the Murray bid is a bit of a joke."

But Marion was clear. "There's no reason why they can't do it, and they're local. All round, it would be far more satisfactory. They could start earlier, albeit on a smaller scale, and everything would be kept local. It's true that we'd make less money, but it feels right."

He considered her plan, and although he trusted her judgement, he was still unconvinced. "Well, we'd have to speak to Murray to be sure he can do this."

"Yes, I agree." She added, "He's coming over tonight, at about nine."

The washing-up was finished and they made their way through to the den and sat by the fire. It was just after half-past eight.

"Did you notice the bit about the hotel? About us owning half of it?" Jack asked.

"Yes, McAllister's taken advantage of your aunt's death. He's not made a payment for nearly a year."

"Well, I've been in it twice since we arrived and I haven't seen a soul in there other than a few locals."

The Quartermaster

She answered impatiently, "Well, *obviously*. It is January, after all. Businesses like McAllister's make nearly all their money in the spring and summer seasons. Although, from what I can see from the books, the last few seasons haven't been very good."

At a few seconds to nine o'clock a sharp ring at the door signalled the arrival of Murray. Marion, who was now leading this project, rose to answer the call. A moment later she returned with Murray and an extra chair.

Murray did not look like a multinational company. He was tall, slim and his cherubic face was clean shaven. He wore suit trousers and a collar and tie. His hair was short, blond and neatly cut. Jack doubted he was more than twenty.

The additional chair was supplemented by a lightweight card table, and all three sat down around it. James Murray accepted the drink Jack offered but, Jack noted, had the confidence to alert Jack that he was being over-generous with the spirit while pouring.

The purpose of the small table quickly became clear, and Murray reached into a small case and produced three documents. He wisely opened his pitch by addressing his immediate and obvious weakness.

"I expect you're both surprised at my age," he said. "The truth is, I would much rather not be in this position, but my father died suddenly last year and I had to take over." He paused and looked skyward, perhaps reacting to a brief intrusion of melancholy. "I was in my final year at college when it happened, so I had to come back. Of course, it was always intended that I take over the company – it's been in the family for years – just that the timing was unexpected."

With this concise personal background summary concluded, Murray moved to more comfortable territory and handed out three neatly assembled presentations. He opened his own copy and invited them to do the same. Page by page, the content was reviewed. Taken together, it provided a coherent and persuasive account of how Murray Construction would exploit the resources of the rock.

As the presentation proceeded, Jack warmed to the intense young man before him. He raised his eyes and caught Marion's glance once or twice, and he could tell from her expression that she was also impressed.

As the final page was turned, James Murray said, "Well, thanks very much for giving me the chance to meet with you both. I hope I've covered all the main points." He added candidly, "I am quite aware that there are more experienced firms bidding for this work, but if you choose us, I can guarantee it'll be our most important contract and it'll get all our attention. Have you got any questions?"

In these surroundings, this closing speech could have seemed overly formal, yet his professionalism and obvious sincerity precluded any such reaction.

Jack did not really have any questions, having now gone over to Marion's view that engaging Murray's firm was the right move. However, he felt that the lack of intelligent enquiry would somehow display a lack of interest, so he jumped in and sought clarifications on aspects of the cash flows and financial statements that formed the appendices to the report.

The answers were clear and persuasive, as Jack had expected. Then Jack thought of a better question.

"What's your view on Sunday working?"

James Murray thought for a moment. "Well, this business is very capital intensive and I can't deny that it makes sense to minimise machine downtime. However, Mr Edwards, although I'm not a Free Presbyterian myself, most folks are around here and I respect that. So," he concluded, "I've worked my figures to avoid Sunday working. I calculate that by working an extra hour every day and perhaps two extra each day in the summer, we can make up the time."

He stopped and looked at Jack.

"Yes, sounds good."

As Marion was engaged in some detailed questioning on other financial aspects of the proposal, Jack made his way over to the drinks. "Would you like another drink, Mr Murray?"

"No, thank you. I'd prefer to get back – that is, if you have no more questions. I've been on the go since seven this morning."

This time there were no more questions and Murray left, having once again thanked them for their time and attention, giving them both a formal handshake.

Once he had left, Jack leant back on his chair, pulled hard on a cigarette and conceded, "Well, of course, you were dead right. I reckon he'd do a first-class job. I'm meant to see Sutherland next Friday, but if you're happy, I'll bring it forward and put an end to all the speculation."

Chapter 23

At about ten o'clock, Jack sat on the floorboards of the topmost room in the house, exhausted. As he looked around at the two rough chairs and the small writing desk he had lifted up the stairs over the last two hours, he admitted the result was a poor reward for such exertion. Still, he had some music, a decent speaker, some cigarettes and coffee, so he was happy. A few books would help, and there was a bottle of brandy downstairs.

He went down. Marion was coming from another area of the house and they met. They had been in Mascar for a few days only, but it seemed to Jack that their relationship had changed completely. Each of them seemed to totally understand the other, and despite allowing each other to follow their own day-to-day activities, they had become closer. Each time they encountered each other, it was powerful and stimulating. He instinctively reached for her, catching her round the waist, and, as she feigned to break free, the moment heightened. They gambolled around the landing for a few frenzied seconds until he held her against the wall with playful aggression.

They kissed a few times.

"You seem happy," she said.

"I am. Very." He kissed her again.
She looked at him.
"You okay? Something on your mind?"
"Well, yes, actually there is."
"Out with it."
She looked at him anxiously and hesitated.
He smiled. "Come on."
"I'm pregnant."

Jack was a few years from forty, and he'd received a few shocks in that time but never, ever anything like this. Being told that he had no parents, that if he didn't stop drinking he would die. And then the endless students with their endless problems. He had heard everything, but this was different.

She was waiting. Marion was the strongest, most self-reliant person Jack knew, but when he looked at her, he saw that this time she needed his reaction.

His heart filled with emotions that he had never felt. He panicked momentarily. It was all too perfect: a new life, money, a fabulous house and now this. He was hardly a role model for anyone. He was exploding with joy. Once or twice, in a few of his many idle moments, he had wondered about parenthood, but he always thought it wouldn't happen. And now it was here. He was as nervous as a kitten, but now he wanted it as badly as he had ever wanted anything in his life.

He took a sharp breath, still clinging to her tightly. The first words would be crucial. They would be remembered forever. He didn't want to be clumsy but he had to hurry. She was waiting.

Words wouldn't come, so he held her tighter, tighter than he'd ever held anyone. She responded and they held the embrace for minutes. He unburied his head and, overwhelmed, simply said, "Thank you."

Her features relaxed and she kissed him gently. Then she flicked his nose playfully. "Come on now, we can't stand here all day. These boxes are cluttering up the hall. I'll give you a hand."

With those words she bent over and lifted one of the bulging crates. Ten minutes ago, he would have welcomed her assistance, but now he was horrified.

He ran the few steps to her, supported the box and prised it from her grip. "No, no," he said firmly. "You're exempt from this sort of work now."

She laughed. "Don't be silly."

"I want to be silly," Jack countered, and insisted on struggling up the stairs with the succession of boxes, refusing all offers of assistance.

Lightened by his euphoria, he cleared the hall quickly and soon resumed his place in his new study. All aspects of the work were now pleasurable to him and he made rapid progress. Quite soon the room was bursting with his possessions, and he began to unsystematically place items in different positions, testing the overall effect.

Marion was working downstairs, and he had not seen her for close on half an hour. He felt anxious, so went searching for her.

He found her in the kitchen. He made to utter something but he checked himself. She was deep in conversation with Amanda, who was wearing an expression as downcast as his was exultant.

Marion made a faint "go easy" gesture to him.

He sat down and vaguely remembered something Marion had said last night about Amanda's father. For the second time in an hour, he searched hard for appropriate opening words.

Amanda looked up. "Hello."

"Hello, good journey?"

"Yes, fine."

"I don't suppose you'll feel like any work, in that case."

She countered sharply. "I don't see why we shouldn't work. I'm here, aren't I?"

Jack felt his clumsiness acutely. "Yes, of course. Sorry. If you want to do a couple of hours, then fine."

Amanda said, "Well, I don't feel like working, as it happens."

"Okay, but I've got to go to Inverness tomorrow to see my lawyer. Perhaps you'd like to come, and I'll buy you some lunch."

She relaxed a little. "Yes, let's do that."

She disappeared upstairs and Jack said to Marion, "You don't mind, do you? I mean about taking Amanda. She looked as if she needs a lift."

"No, of course I don't mind. Best thing for her."

"Why, what's up with her?"

"She'll tell you."

A different piece of news occurred to Jack. "Have you told Amanda that you're pregnant?"

"No, but I don't mind if you do."

He beamed, walked back, and kissed her again. "Let's go to bed."

Chapter 24

The next morning Amanda was up and ready and seemed a bit brighter, although throughout the journey to Inverness she said little, and it was a relief to Jack when they arrived at the outskirts of the town. He parked near Sutherland's office and got out of the car.

She did not come out of the car. He knocked on the window and she lowered it.

"Come on."

"Are you sure you want me to come? I could wait here until after your meeting."

He had grown a little tired of this – so far unexplained, and uncharacteristic – meekness. "If that arse Sutherland can know all about my business, I don't see why you shouldn't. Come on."

This statement prised her from the car without further comment and a short walk took them to the lawyer's office.

As they entered the foyer, Sutherland was emerging from his room to consult with his receptionist. He nodded curtly in Jack's direction, although Jack noted that his expression brightened when his gaze lingered over Amanda.

Sutherland returned to his office and, some minutes later, re-emerged, escorting a very small and elderly lady on his arm, all the time uttering oily, benevolent platitudes as he escorted her to the door. Once she was despatched, he turned and, in a close to peremptory fashion, beckoned Jack to come through.

"This is Miss Barratt, a business associate," Jack said.

Sutherland eyed Amanda cautiously and moved behind his oversized desk. "Well, Mr Edwards, I understand that you've had some further thoughts on the quarry," he purred.

"Yes, I've decided that we should definitely reopen it."

Sutherland smiled. "A very wise decision, Mr Edwards. Now it only remains to decide on whether to give the work to Thompson or Peters." He consulted a file. "My recommendation is for Thompson. Their terms are slightly better and they've got slightly more experience. However, Peters is an excellent company, with exciting plans."

"Are they both British companies?" Jack asked.

Sutherland scowled and had to dip into his folder again. "They are both PLCs. Thompson is headquartered in the UK, in London, but Peters is Swedish. Is this important?"

Jack said airily, "Well, we would want to do the most we can for the local community."

"Yes, of course. That would seem to tip the balance towards Thompson."

"I had a talk with Marion last night. We've decided."

"Thompson or Peters?"

"Murray," Jack answered casually.

"Murray?" the lawyer repeated, screwing his brow to recall the name. A comfortable smile broke over his features. "Murray are just small local builders. Maybe they've done a bit of quarrying but I'm not sure. It's not a serious bid."

"Have you reviewed their submission?"

"Yes, ages ago," Sutherland said, "but I didn't take it forward. I mean they can't possibly undertake a project on this scale. No, it'll have to be either Thompson or Peters."

"No, it's to be Murray. We've spoken to their managing director and both Marion and I are convinced that they're the right choice."

"The managing director? But Bob Murray's dead!"

"Not Bob Murray, his son James. He's the managing director now."

"James?" repeated Sutherland, his voice growing shriller. "He's still at college. What does he know about quarrying?"

"Quite a bit, actually," Jack said laconically and added, to interrupt Sutherland's anticipated next protest, "So it's decided, and I've agreed with Mr Murray that he can start preliminary work immediately. I'll need all the technical reports and accounts relating to the quarry now, and draft contracts if they're ready."

Sutherland fiddled with his pen and took a deep breath. "It would be wise to undertake a further short assessment for you, simply to ensure that nothing has been overlooked in the Murray submission. I could arrange that for you."

"No," Jack said. "We want to go with Murray."

"There are legal and health and safety requirements that must be—"

But Sutherland didn't get to finish.

"Please listen, Mr Sutherland," Amanda said politely. "It's Mr fucking Murray."

Chapter 25

Marion pulled on her Barbour and went out of the door, buckling a little as the force of the wet wind caught her. She returned to the alcove, picked up a large umbrella and, with difficulty, forced it outward against the gale. This done, she was well clad against the elements, and the short walk to the cliff path and down to the village proved pleasurable despite the tempest.

She stopped outside the hotel and, after steeling herself, turned into the main foyer and into a small reception area. This area was dominated by a large working desk. As she moved towards it, she noted a small office beyond it. On her left there was an arrangement of tired furnishings, save for the impressive fireplace that was disappointingly rendered redundant, masked by the functional and unattractive gas fire.

To her right there was a small corridor to an opaque glazed door which was marked "Public Bar". After a wait of a minute, she rang a bell on the desk. Still no one came. A little exasperated, she headed into the public bar. It, too, was empty but, before she could decide on her next move, she heard footsteps behind her and turned in time to see the florid features of McAllister filling the narrow passageway.

He was smiling and he extended his hand.

"Hello," he said cordially. "Are you Mrs Edwards?"

Marion laughed. "Not exactly. Just call me Marion."

"Yes, fine. I hope you've not been waiting long. I've been down in the cellar and I thought my wife would be here." He made a mock gesture with his head and eyes as if searching for his wife under the chairs and tables until, satisfied that she was not there, he said, "We can go up to the sitting room to talk."

He led the way through a door past the artificial fireplace and she followed him up the stairs. The carpets were wearing, the wallpaper no longer achieved comprehensive coverage and the whole place smelled a bit. A little way down the corridor they arrived at a door marked "Private"

The McAllisters' private sitting room was a depressing place. It was small and untidy and was dominated by a large colour television that was showing an afternoon soap opera. Almost invisible, lying along the covered sofa, was a woman who, although it was early afternoon, still wore a robe. She was small and grey, about fifty years old, had a glass of whisky in her hand, and looked about as bad as anyone outside a hospital ward could.

The soap opera was absorbing all of her attention and she made no move on their arrival. Marion stood near the doorway while McAllister conducted an urgent but futile tidying effort, moving quickly around the small room, picking up discarded newspapers and a couple of dirty plates. He gave up and looked embarrassed, then moved smartly across to the television. With an aggressive flourish, he switched it off. This, at last, roused the woman.

She cursed loudly at McAllister. "It's nearly bloody finished. What the hell did you do that for?"

McAllister did not answer. His head moved in Marion's direction. The woman jerked violently and stared at Marion.

She lifted her head and without obvious embarrassment or abandoning her prone position said, "Who's she?"

McAllister's face reddened. "This is Marion. Mr Edward's partner."

Marion said, "Look, if it's not convenient at the moment we can talk later."

"It's perfectly convenient now," Mrs McAllister said coldly. "What do you want?"

"Well, I wanted to have a word with you about the hotel. I'll be helping him manage things."

McAllister sat down beside his wife on the sofa. "Have a seat, Marion."

He indicated a single armchair facing the sofa. The armchair was covered with a filthy white throw. From the smell, Marion deduced that its purpose was to protect the upholstery from the attentions of a dog. In this case, the cure was worse than the disease, and Marion sat ill at ease, the McAllisters looking at her intently.

Such unconvivial surroundings at least ensured that there would be little small talk. Marion asked weakly, "How's business?"

McAllister shrugged. "Not bad. Better in the summer obviously. Sometimes we get parties, walkers, that sort of thing."

"I understand from our records that about a year ago a loan was granted to you by Mr Edwards' late aunt – fifty thousand pounds – for the purposes of refurbishment." She paused, thinking that from what she had already seen, this money had certainly been wasted.

McAllister said sharply, "Aye, well, Miss Edwards was always keen to help out. She said that we should pay it back when we could. It was all fairly informal."

Marion looked at him. It was a pointless lie, but it helped her to keep things business-like. She pulled a letter out of her bag and read the key paragraph. "The principal to be repaid monthly over a period of not more than five years." She returned the paper to her bag and looked at them. "As far as I can see no repayments have yet been made."

McAllister said sullenly, "Aye, well it's been difficult."

Marion waited, but it seemed that this was the only explanation that would be forthcoming. She suppressed a wave of anger. Maybe she should have waited a while to broach the subject. She said coldly, "I think we should talk about this another time. When suits you?"

McAllister's expression softened a little. "Yes, thanks, let's do that."

Marion rose from the foul armchair. "In a week or so?"

And then the eruption happened. Mrs McAllister's pale and thin features exploded in misery. She raised her small head skyward, sneered and snarled, "What kind of a man are you, Jim McAllister? Sitting there, begging to her. Just pay her and get rid of her."

McAllister looked angrily at his wife, but it didn't stop her.

She then turned to Marion. "And you, sitting talking to us like that with your city airs. Who do you think you are? Probably think you're something special, living in that big house. Come to help us, I suppose? Give us the benefit of your experience? Why don't you go and leave us alone?"

Marion said haughtily, "Yes, I'm going to do that, Mrs McAllister. Good morning."

Mrs McAllister wasn't finished. She sprang off the sofa. Dipping into the drawer of a bookcase, she emerged holding a fistful of bank notes. She waved them at Marion. "We're about a year behind. At a thousand a month, that's twelve thousand pounds?"

Marion watched as she threw the bank notes on the sofa and then began counting them out.

McAllister went to her and muttered something in her ear, but she shrugged him off violently. "Let's just pay her."

Marion stood frozen in the doorway. She thought about saying something, but words would be useless.

Mrs McAllister was a fast counter. Holding a bunch of fifty-pound notes, she walked towards Marion malevolently and banged them down on a table. "There you are – twelve thousand pounds. Do you want to count it?"

Marion shook her head.

Mrs McAllister produced a carrier bag and swept the cash into it. Twisting it to seal it, she thrust it at Marion." Now will you leave us alone?"

Marion thought about returning the bag but decided not to. Keeping the money would, at least, postpone any further meeting. "Thank you, Mrs McAllister, good morning."

She turned on her heels and headed back down the stairs. There were steps behind her but she didn't stop. She wasn't interested in any platitudes or apologies and stayed ahead until she reached the exit door. Clear of the place, she turned. McAllister was standing behind her, but from the expression on his face, it didn't look as if he had been intending to apologise.

Chapter 26

After her robust putting down of the lawyer, and a couple of drinks over a quick lunch, Amanda's spirits had improved a little, and she was more talkative on the return journey.

"So, can I ask what happened in London?" Jack asked.

"Yes, of course you can ask," she said enigmatically.

A few more miles along the desolate road passed before she started to talk. Jack listened in silence and the dark and sombre silhouetted hills provided an appropriate backdrop to her story.

When they returned to the house it was dusk, but as he got out of the car and through the gloom, he noticed that the McRae brothers had made good their promises of yesterday.

Leaving Amanda, he walked round to the side of the house. They were tidying up, loading things into an ancient transit van.

Ian McRae said, "Evening, Mr Edwards. That's us just finished. We've re-felted both of these garages. That should do them for a while."

"That looks a good job," Jack said encouragingly. "What about the old barn?"

"I've had a look at it, but it's a bigger job. Needs new joists, although the stonework's okay. You want us to do that?"

"Yes, go ahead, and what about that scaffolding?

"The stonework's done but there's a little bit of roofing to be done, a week or so."

"Fine, just keep going. Now what about money? You want cash?"

"If you've got it. Say five hundred for today? I'll let you know about the barn and the roofing work, but it might be a couple of thousand."

Jack didn't mean to look flashy, but he had been to the bank in town and withdrawn a lot of cash in anticipation. He peeled off ten fifty-pound notes.

McRae took the money and added it to a larger bundle of notes which he produced from his pocket, "We'll be back tomorrow."

Jack returned to the house and headed for the kitchen, which was fast becoming the hub of his home. He opened a wine bottle and announced, "I've just paid off the McRae brothers. They've made a good start on those outbuildings."

Such an inconsequential remark was, however, destined to pass unremarked upon. As he looked down, he saw that Amanda was sitting at the table close to Marion, holding her arm.

"What is it?" Jack asked urgently.

"Marion's had some kind of row with the hotel owner, McAllister."

Jack moved Amanda aside and held Marion, who was slowly raising her bowed head. She wasn't crying but was resisting his gaze.

"What happened?"

She indicated the carrier bag on the table.

Jack picked it up, looked inside and tipped out the contents onto the table. He picked up some of the bank notes. "There's about ten thousand pounds here."

"Twelve, apparently," Marion said. "It's the full arrears on the hotel loan."

"Nice."

"No, it wasn't *nice*. It wasn't *nice* at all." She described the earlier scene with McAllister and his wife.

Jack was furious. "Bloody nerve. The cheeky bastards live at our expense and then this."

"I'm sure I just caught her on a bad day. They'll be incredibly apologetic tomorrow, you'll see. Besides, we've got the money."

Jack said thoughtfully, "Yes, we've got the money. Pretty impressive to have twelve thousand pounds in a drawer, but dammit, I'm not having it. I'm going down there now."

"No, don't do that, Jack. Please leave it."

"Look, I'll stay calm, but I'm not having this. We can't start on this basis. I promise I won't make a scene."

Marion sighed and appealed to Amanda, who shrugged.

"I'll be back soon."

***

As he entered the bar, there was no sign of McAllister. His wife was there, however, and she was sitting on a stool at the end of the bar, laughing heartily with several companions and obviously in good spirits. It was annoying, but Jack was too old-fashioned to confront a woman in public, and he meekly went to the opposite end of the bar and waited.

He did not have to wait long for the tuneless whistling that drifted from behind the bar area to grow louder. McAllister emerged. He was in a good mood, too.

McAllister stopped whistling when he caught sight of Jack. "Oh, hello."

Jack didn't bother with an opening pleasantry. "Can I have a word with you, please?"

McAllister sidled up in a mock conspiratorial way.

But Jack wasn't laughing. "No, not here, somewhere more private."

McAllister's face lengthened and he led Jack out of the bar and into the small office behind the main reception desk. "Have a seat."

"No, I'll stand. It'll not take long. I've just left Marion and she was upset." He raised his voice. "What the hell do you think you're doing?"

McAllister shrugged. "Look, my wife was a bit aggressive, but you've got your money, so what's the problem?"

"The fucking problem is there's no reason that Marion should be spoken to like that."

McAllister moved a bit nearer. "Well, these things happen. We're all a bit stressed these days."

McAllister's face was a little too close to Jack's now, but neither pulled back.

"These things might happen, but I'd be grateful if they didn't again."

McAllister looked at him and then took a step back, laughing. "Aye, okay, anything you say, Jack."

Chapter 27

It was nearly ten o'clock and Kate Phillips removed her spectacles, put her hands to her head and rubbed her face vigorously. The inspectors had retired to their hotel for the night after subjecting her to an exhausting day.

The little fat man had taken no great part in the audit and had been assigned the most junior of roles, fetching and carrying files and taking messages from the others to her staff. It would not continue. Today was no more than an exercise in familiarisation with the workings of the bank. Tomorrow would be different. He would sit alone, examining whatever he chose, and the others would do the fetching and carrying.

She was confident that they had found nothing so far. They had, as she had anticipated, started by examining a selection of those large accounts with significant foreign exchange transactions. None of her special accounts had been selected, although they might have been but for her early morning visit.

They had undertaken their work with good humour and had, at the end of the day, invited her back to the hotel for drinks. She had declined.

She reclined in her chair and closed her eyes, but a moment later, she rose and opened the ornate doors in the centre of an impressive wooden bureau that stood against the wall opposite. She fiddled with the remote control and hopped through the television's offerings until she stopped at a news bulletin.

Someone was being interviewed. A spokesman, they called him. In turn, he accused opponents of bad faith and duplicity, ending with a hint of menace as he warned of the potential consequences of not getting his way.

Kate knew him. She hated everything he stood for, but she didn't hate *him*. Even although, all those years ago, it was he and his kind who had killed them. It was because of them that, all those years ago, the policeman and the policewoman had come to the door of the little terraced house. That was a long time ago.

She wondered if she was like him. He was prepared to fight for his beliefs and was indefatigable in promoting them. As long as he had breath, he would fight for his cause. Until the British were out and the island united, he couldn't stop. He continued in measured tones, but Kate knew he was right. If you didn't get what you wanted, and you wanted it badly enough, then you had to kill people.

From the inside of her case a new disposable mobile phone rang. She recognised the number but didn't welcome it. She listened. The news wasn't good.

"You told us you had everything under control," she said.

"Well, we're probably all right, but it's not worth taking the risk."

"How long have we got?"

"Maybe a week."

"No, no, you need to get us two weeks. Do whatever you need, anything, but get me two weeks." She threw the mobile back into the case, and locked it.

A couple of swear words seemed appropriate and she delivered them. As she did so, she became aware of the beginnings of faint noise from the door. Gingerly at first and then more confidently, the large brass knob turned, followed by the gradual opening of the door.

She stared at the widening aperture until it was filled. She looked straight into the hard eyes of Frank Barras.

If he was shocked by finding her sitting behind her desk, he did not show it, and his voice, when it came, betrayed no sign of nerves, just sufficiently flavoured with the mild embarrassment one might feel on entering another's room uninvited.

Through his round glasses he peered at her and he gave a slight smile. "I'm sorry, I thought you would have gone by now. I'm afraid I've been rather stupid and left my briefcase somewhere. Very careless of me."

Careless, my foot. "Come in, Mr Barras," she said.

He moved into the office and peered around for a few obligatory seconds before declaring, in a deprecating voice, "Oh, here it is. Silly of me."

He apologised again and made to leave, clinging to his case with exaggerated relief, but she halted him. "No harm done. As you and I are the only ones still working, have a seat. How about a drink?"

"Why not? It's been a tiring day."

"So, how are you getting on? Are you getting everything you need?"

"Yes, thank you. Your staff have been very attentive and efficient. Pity your secretary didn't make it in today."

Kate looked at him closely. "Have you worked in compliance long?"

Barras yawned and took a mouthful of whisky. "Oh, years! Well, at least that's what it feels like."

"Things must have changed a good deal?"

"Yes, so many changes. It's exhausting. It's all new computer systems and new buzzwords these days. To be honest, I can't really keep up. I'm due for retirement in a few years so I just tag along with some of the teams. Give them the benefit of my experience – that is, if they listen."

Kate looked at him flopped in the armchair and thought how easy it would have been to accept his account. His thick glasses, his untidy appearance, his slow speech and his benign lack of ambition completed the mask.

Only once did the mask slip. As he leant over to place his drink on the small table she had moved to his side, his glasses fell, and as he recovered them, he sat up. They caught each other's gaze full on. His deep-set, pale eyes were alert and penetrating, and for a moment, they opened a window into his soul and she saw just how dangerous he was. He refused her offer of another drink, laughing and saying that at his time of life he could no longer stand the late nights, and he left, once again apologising for his intrusion.

When he had gone, she picked up his glass and idled across the room. Barras was a professional. Leaving the case was a nice touch and easy to explain away. But why was he returning to her office? She didn't like it. Either to place a bug or to engage in a simple search. Either way, it was clear she was being investigated.

Her thoughts returned to the telephone conversation that she had not had time to consider before Barras's interruption. She laughed. It was ironic that the supposedly difficult part of the operation had passed off smoothly and this current period of planned inaction had become awkward.

She clasped her hands in front of her and thought hard, biting into her top lip, but she didn't panic. She never panicked. That was why she was the boss.

Chapter 28

When Jack got up the next day, the sun was shining through the curtains. He yawned and reached over for Marion, but she wasn't there, which was fair enough as it was after ten. He stretched again and felt well. Today was going to be a good day, a chance to expunge a few unpleasant memories of the previous day. Hamish was coming over to walk some hills. But first: young James Murray, to whom Jack would have the pleasurable task of entrusting with the reopening of the quarry.

Jack sprang out of bed and went downstairs. He poked his nose in all the ground-floor rooms until he found Marion in the study.

She looked up. "At last. I was just about to come and get you. Murray's due here soon."

He moved alongside her. She was surrounded by documents. Unusually, she was smartly dressed, with a little make-up and a hint of scent. He kissed her neck. "You look nice. First time I've seen you in business clothes for a while."

She laughed. "Well, it's not for you. It's for Mr Murray. If he takes the trouble to be so business-like in his dealings with us, I thought we could reciprocate, at least for one day. At least one of us needs to make an effort." She pushed him away

The Quartermaster

and began gathering up the papers. "Stop it, he's due to be here soon, and you know how punctual he is."

As she had predicted, Murray was on time and, as anticipated, was thrilled when told he had been selected. "Thanks, Mrs Edwards, you won't regret this. I plan to start some preliminary work in the next few days."

Marion laughed and said, "I'm sure we're going to see a lot of each other from now on. So, it's Marion and Jack."

James nodded shyly. "I'm going to take a walk up there now. I need to take a few photographs. Do you want to come along?"

"Yes, why not?" Marion said. "Jack?"

"Yes, Hamish is not due for an hour or so."

He looked out of the window. The weather seemed set fair, and after Marion had quickly changed out of her suit and back into jeans and boots, they set out on the walk.

"There's a track up there, brings you into the quarry from the top of the hill," James said. "Or would you rather drive?"

Nobody wanted to drive, but Jack wished that they had, as the walk proved deceptively long and the rude path was uneven and boggy.

A pleasant distraction was, however, provided by James's enthusiasm and expert observations of the local flora and fauna. At another of the seemingly endless local high points, the workings and the tops of the outbuildings of the quarry came into view.

James was enthusiastic and said, with an expression of pride and sadness, "My father used to work here."

Jack looked around. The cliff face was smooth and scarred and below there were four rusting storage containers, a couple of workman's huts and a lot of miscellaneous rusting equipment lying around. "It's a bit of an eyesore, to be frank."

"Oh, I'll have this all tidied up soon," James said. "This is the original seam. It was exhausted some five years ago, but if you follow me round …" He gestured and led them around an outcrop. "That's where we'll start. There's at least twenty years here."

Marion seemed more interested in this than Jack and asked him a question that sounded contractual. Jack looked at his watch. It was nearly eleven. He excused himself and began to walk back alone.

Chapter 29

It was best to park the car well short of the entrance to the main track, where the layby dipped over a rise and rendered the vehicle invisible from the road. It meant a half mile over the rough ground and an indirect route to the quarry, but it wasn't a bad day, and the gentle downhill walk was easy.

Just past the quarry face, in through a hidden recess in the rock, the metal door seemed secure. The padlock wasn't, however. It sat on the ground, the shank cut through cleanly.

The metal door gave easily without sound and, after a further, careful few yards through a cladding-free rocky passageway and into a small storage area, all was not well.

The trap door was open and there was a man on his knees gazing down. He didn't look round; he was engrossed in the view. Then he disappeared from sight into the chasm below. Sounds of an investigation came from below, but it didn't last long, and the man's head emerged at ground level. He stared at the newcomer, looked puzzled and made to speak, but there wasn't really anything to talk about. The man's head jerked back as it absorbed the kick, and he fell backwards and back down into the pit.

The pit was only about six-feet deep, but the man had landed on the edge of one of the packing crates. There wasn't a lot of blood but there was a severe depression where his left temple used to be. He wasn't breathing.

The dead man was a complication but not a priority, and each of the crates was examined closely and reconciled with the list. Everything was accounted for and, with an effort, the dead man was forced upwards onto the floor. The trapdoor was replaced and a miscellaneous range of debris spread on top of it.

The dead man needed to be moved outside and be found there. He would be missed, and a search would be unwelcome. Dragging the body was easier than lifting, but that task also had to be delayed.

The woman who entered the area did a little better than the man. She managed to utter a sound and, at the same time, turn on her heel and run out of the storage area.

She seemed fit and fast, difficult to overtake.

Luck was more important than skill, and the first shot caught her high in her back, just short of the metal door. She fell face forward. Then she twitched and a second bullet finished things.

Chapter 30

Jack's journey down the hill proved more interesting than he might have imagined, and he put his newly acquired knowledge of his surroundings to the test. As he walked back, the house eventually came into view. Though by now he could see the final approaches of the cliff road, there was no sign of Hamish's car.

He needed cigarettes and decided to head to the shop.

He passed the hotel, which was closed, and the terraced houses were silent. Miss Crawford's shop door was firmly shut also, and a small sign ill-placed at about knee level told him that service would resume in five minutes.

He decided to wait. He crossed the road and sat on the sea wall, enjoying a peaceful moment before a large vehicle roared into the village and stopped at the hotel. Someone got out. A man, but Jack didn't see who. It might have been McAllister, but he didn't want to see McAllister after yesterday's exchanges. He turned his head back out to sea and waited.

When he returned to Miss Crawford's shop, it was open. He purchased cigarettes.

"Oh, I meant to say," she said. "I generally get deliveries on Wednesday and fresh vegetables and fruit, so I will have most of these things that you wanted then."

"Yes, thanks."

He made to leave. She said, "Such good news about you reopening the quarry."

How the hell did she know that? They'd only decided yesterday. He turned back round to face her and said, rather testily, "Well, thank goodness the Mascar grapevine is alive and flourishing."

She was a little taken aback and, he thought, a little upset at this reply. "Sorry," he added in a smoother and more conciliatory tone." "Yes, you're quite right. James Murray will be starting work soon."

Her smile returned. "I'm sorry, I didn't mean to pry, only, well, it's such good news for the local area and," she confessed, "I'm afraid that most people know."

No doubt they did, thought Jack, and he returned her smile weakly.

Although he did not particularly care for Crawford, he felt a little sorry for her. She was trying really hard, making a colossal effort to blend into the area, but it just didn't work. Her attitudes were intellectually formed rather than assembled from living or doing. That wasn't her fault, of course, but it just wasn't the same. Unless she acknowledged this truth, Jack knew she would always struggle. He wondered if he should say something like this, but he didn't really care enough and decided not to.

When he left the shop, as before, the street was deserted. The car that had been outside the hotel was gone. He looked up to the house. Hamish wasn't there either.

He decided on a whim to pay an unannounced visit to the Reverend McCallum. He might not be welcome, but he didn't care. McCallum had barged in on Jack, so he could have no complaints.

At the junction at the end of the village, a small, overgrown track branched off the road, and a pleasant walk through trees and undergrowth led to the manse. The house was well-sized with close-set conifers marking its boundary. Its exterior white paintwork was peeling a bit, but the overall effect was striking. Also, in contrast to the general lack of richness of the surrounding land, the gardens were comparatively verdant, like an oasis in the desert. He arrived at a rotting wooden fence and then an even more rotten gate, which had collapsed, its bottom right-hand corner sitting on the ground. Jack needed to lift it slightly before he could push it back. It was even more flimsy than it had looked, and despite his modest application of force, it chose to abandon its hinges completely and collapse miserably to the ground.

The collapsing gate wasn't his fault, but he felt awkward and looked furtively to the house and then around the grounds to confirm that he had acted unseen. Satisfied that he had, he bent down, lifted the wooden gate and was engaged in effecting invisible repairs when he was disturbed by McCallum, who had, with bad timing, emerged silently from the side of the house.

He wore his full clerical uniform, but his lower half was protected by a rough-looking apron and he sported a large pair of bright-red gardening gloves. His expression was more surprised than stern when he recognised his clumsy visitor was Jack, and he greeted him in neutral tones while casting an eye to his gate.

"I'm afraid I may have damaged your gate."

"Oh, leave it, it's been rotten for years and it's always falling down. Actually, I use this gate here as the main access." McCallum pointed out a large – and now more obvious – entranceway. He led Jack around the house and into a large and dilapidated greenhouse. "I hope you don't mind" – he indicated the plants and pots before him – "but these cuttings can't wait. It'll just take a few moments."

Jack stood silently and watched as the fearsome cleric lovingly and with surprising dexterity handled the cuttings: as promised, within a few minutes they were all tended and carefully potted.

He reviewed them one last time and turned to Jack. Resuming his familiar formality, he said, "Well, what can I do for you, Mr Edwards?"

Jack cleared his throat. "I thought that after our recent discussions I would like to inform you of progress on the quarry. It seems there are no secrets around here so I thought I'd tell you myself. The fact is we've decided that, for the overall good of the community, we should reopen it."

McCallum looked severe but Jack continued and didn't allow any interruption. "We've awarded the contract to James Murray and he has agreed that it would be in the best interests of all if Sunday working is not permitted."

McCallum's expression eased. He said pompously, "I must congratulate you on this decision. I'm sure it's for the best."

Jack did not give a toss about the issues that were of obvious importance to McCallum, and he didn't like the way that McCallum would, doubtless, present the decision as his own triumph, but he didn't care.

McCallum retained his austere façade, but as Jack went out, stepping over the still prone wooden gate, he heard a faint sound of whistling from the greenhouse. This, Jack thought, represented the measure of his own victory.

Chapter 31

So far it had been a satisfactory morning. Murray was already proving an inspired choice, and, against the odds, he had squared McCallum.

He regained the main road just as Hamish's Volvo came into view. It screamed to a halt well onto the verge. "Get in!" Hamish shouted.

The car was filthy and it wasn't just the dogs to blame. It was true that, when travelling, they were unconfined and allowed to roam freely, but even without their influence, the interior was a disgrace. "This car could do with a clean."

"Yes, I keep meaning to do that," Hamish said cheerfully.

Hamish might have emptied the ashtray once, but Jack doubted it. And now it didn't matter. The car would be scrapped long before the overflow capacity of the passenger leg area was filled up. As Jack shuffled his feet gingerly, further examination of the footwell revealed an assortment of bottles and cans representing an impressive range of market brands. Some had been drained before being tossed aside, but others not, and as Jack shuffled, his feet seeking sanctuary, the movement upset one of the cans and its contents seeped out. But it didn't really matter: the numerous newspapers and fast-food wrappers provided suitable absorbents.

Surprisingly, however, the miscellaneous malodorous debris when combined neutralised the overall effect, for the car smelled pleasant and, although the dogs did their best, the atmosphere was faintly appealing and not nauseating.

Hamish was in a good mood and talked continually on the short drive. As he approached the worst corner on the road, he stubbed out his cigarette in the overflowing ashtray. As the car lurched around the corner, several butts fell out.

When they got into the house, only Amanda was in residence.

"Any sign of Marion and James?" Jack asked.

"No, although I'm not long up."

Jack wasn't all that happy. He knew why that was. Twenty-four hours ago, he would have been unconcerned, but knowing she was pregnant changed things.

"Will we head off?" Hamish asked.

"Let's have a coffee first. I want to see Marion. She should be back soon."

Three coffees later, there was still no sign of her, and the conversation had stalled. Amanda was also exhibiting signs of preoccupation and, Jack noted, she had made no mention of the book. Her preoccupation became more evident when the telephone rang and she visibly started.

Jack, bored, lifted himself without interest and picked up the telephone. It was a man with a well-polished accent. "It's for you, Amanda."

She was through to the hall quickly. Her conversation, however, proved one-sided, and apart from a few routine matters of acknowledgement, she contributed little. It was all over in under a minute. She returned to the kitchen table and resumed her expression of boredom.

"Who was that?" Jack asked.

"Oh, just another client." She was in no mood to provide further information, and after a while, she got up and began to unsystematically assemble items from the pantry and engage in the preparation of lunch.

"We should go soon," Hamish said. "There's only a few hours of daylight at this time of year."

Jack wanted to wait for Marion, but he was being unreasonable now. It was hardly fair to invite someone over and then spend the day sitting around moping. "Okay, we'll have something to eat and then go."

"Fine. What about you, Amanda. You coming with us?"

She sighed. "Why not?"

After a cold meal and a bit of a struggle to find Amanda suitable hillwalking gear, they left the house. Hamish indicated the way and they moved off, following a path of sorts towards two distant peaks still bathed in winter sunshine.

Jack was still fretting about Marion, but decided he was being silly. He should try to enjoy the day. Armed with his binoculars and the little knowledge imparted by Murray earlier on, he concentrated on the local fauna. They made slow progress up the hill, walking in silence with their heads bowed against the freshening wind. The day was otherwise fine, however, and after a little they stopped, rested and enjoyed the views.

The courting ravens croaked noisily as they matched each other in a series of increasingly impressive aerial acrobatics, and Jack raised his binoculars to watch them.

After a moment, they abandoned their love-in and, one following the other, flew quickly across a black crag. It soon became clear what had attracted their attention. The golden eagle that soared effortlessly above the hill was uninvited, and immediate priority had to be given to warning off the unwelcome intruder.

When all three came into Jack's field of vision, the huge differential in the size of the birds convinced him that the ravens had taken on an impossible task. The light caught the face of the eagle, still untroubled, although it allowed itself a deprecatory downward glance at their approach.

The still-croaking corvids knew what they were doing. The first raven concentrated on close quarter work, employing its superior manoeuvrability to make short stabs at the eagle, approaching flat and fast and breaking off at the sight of the massive talons. The eagle still looked indifferent, confident of its ability to ward off such a feeble attack. But its discomfiture increased when the second raven, which had, just before approach, soared high above the eagle, opened a second front and repeatedly began dive-bombing its larger foe.

Again and again they attacked, and a little success was eventually achieved as the eagle, for the first time, was forced to use wing power. Fearing more a loss of dignity than the possibility of injury, it effected a sharp turn and proceeded back in the direction whence it had come with steady, slow and powerful flaps.

The ravens reunited and croaked triumphantly, although they did not accept this reverse as conclusive proof of the eagle's departure. They evidently feared the possibility of an aquiline tactical gambit, and, like two small tugs beside a super-tanker, they escorted the eagle for some minutes until, satisfied, they turned and returned to their home.

As the birds separated, Jack maintained the glass on the eagle and watched as it resumed its effortless glide across the hilltop. It had obviously caught a helpful thermal and was moving so fast that within a minute he had turned 180 degrees.

The bird was over the quarry now, and as he tracked it, a glint of light from a rock made him blink. He removed the binoculars from his eyes for a second. When he returned them to his eyes, the bird had gone, and he searched in vain over and around the blackness of the quarry face. The sun had fallen from its midday peak and was dropping fast behind the quarry. Although it was barely two in the afternoon, the quarry floor was in semi-darkness.

But it wasn't dark enough to conceal the two static forms which Jack's sweep picked out. He stared hard, attempting to focus his eyes. His throat went dry. He couldn't be certain, but he was sure it was two people – and they were lying on the ground, motionless. Sunbathing was out of the question in Mascar, even in the high summer, so what were they doing? He watched for a full minute expecting, at any time, to see some small, reassuring movement, but none came, and his stare grew more rigid until he lost the focus and dropped the glasses.

This brought Hamish across. "Careful with these."

Jack picked them up. "Here, have a look. At the quarry. On the ground, straight down from the highest point of the face."

Hamish took the glasses and scanned. "I can't see anything."

"You're looking in the wrong place, further south, over the knoll."

Brown scanned in the area indicated. The binoculars stopped moving.

"You see?"

Hamish said slowly, "I see something but I can't make it out."

By this time Amanda, growing cold in consequence of the extended stop, became impatient. "What are you looking at?" She made to prise the glasses from Hamish but, without releasing his gaze, he brushed her off with his arm. Then, slowly, his arms dropped and the binoculars with them. Without a word, he passed them to her and turned to Jack. He looked serious. "Maybe we should get a bit nearer."

Amanda also looked serious. "Yes, let's do that."

"What can you see, Amanda?" Jack asked.

Adam Parish

"I don't know. Let's go."

Chapter 32

The quarry was about half a mile away, and as Jack covered the ground, he was continually stumbling and picking himself up. At first, he allowed himself short stops to look through the glasses and seek a better view, but this became impossible as he negotiated a deep U-shaped depression.

His mind raced as fast as his body. On looking back, he saw that, despite his superior conditioning, Hamish was trailing, with Amanda about the same distance further back. He never considered waiting for them and ran on, covering the rough going, recklessly ignoring its hazards. After a number of false summits with which the direct route teased him, at last he embarked on the final ascent. The slope that would take him to the floor of the quarry.

He stood rigid, unable to capture the breath his lungs sought. He raised his head. Two dark, irregular shapes had now materialised, and whatever the scope of his frenzied imaginings while running, the sight that greeted him was worse.

They lay together, close to him, face up with their arms tidily arranged at their sides.

Jack was about twenty yards away, but that was near enough to know that they were both dead. He started to walk forward, every stride in slow motion. And then he stopped. The remainder of the face that used to be Murray was sickening, but it didn't mean anything to Jack. Instead, he moved to her.

She lay with an expression of serenity and calm, her hair evenly and neatly arranged on either side of her face. She looked beautiful; she would always look beautiful. He wanted to move, but he couldn't, and then he did. The muscles in his calves, then his thighs, gave way, and he slowly sank to the ground. Involuntarily, his head slumped into his open hands. The demand of his lungs for breath could no longer be ignored, and it emerged simultaneously with the first wave of shock. He emitted a roar that bounced off the quarry face and across the vast wilderness. Then he fell alongside her and held her lifeless body in his arms. He held her tightly. He was never going to let her go.

A moment later, Amanda and Brown emerged into the quarry floor and stood beside Jack. Brown swore and Amanda, in more control of her emotions, knelt alongside Jack.

He felt Amanda's hand on his shoulder. She was talking to him softly but he couldn't understand what she was saying. She slowly unpicked Jack's arms from Marion. He tried to cling on but he couldn't, and a combination of Amanda and Hamish moved Jack a few yards away from the body.

Jack sat motionless and watched Amanda as she first looked over Murray, his blond hair now curled into his open skull.

Jack tested his legs and they worked. He moved to Amanda, who was fiddling with her mobile. "Fuck!" she exclaimed. "Is there no signal here?"

Hamish looked at her phone. "Same as mine. No signal on this network."

Amanda swore again. "You guys need to leave this to me. Go back to the house." She beckoned to Hamish. "Take Jack back to the house and call the police. Hurry."

Hamish approached and tapped Jack on the arm.

Jack pushed him away roughly. "I'm going nowhere."

"Leave him," Amanda said. "We need the police. Hamish, can you go back?"

Hamish nodded and, without a word, disappeared down the hill.

Jack moved alongside Amanda and watched her.

"Keep behind me," she told him. "We mustn't contaminate the scene." She held him with both arms and shouted, "You must stand still!"

Amanda was finished with Murray and she moved to Marion. Jack followed.

She produced a pair of gloves and turned Marion over. The wounds were obvious. Jack looked away for a second while Amanda looked at her closely. Again, she led Jack a few yards away. "Stay there. Just for a minute. Let me look."

He did what he was told this time and fell heavily onto the ground, while she conducted a careful scan of the area surrounding the bodies.

Jack had a hip flask and he used it now. He downed about half of the contents in a couple of gulps and it worked for a second or two. Then he spluttered and broke into a seemingly endless fit of coughing and dry retching. When he was sure that the fit had passed, he tilted the flask again and emptied it.

The whisky made a difference; he raised his head and, as if by force of will, looked up and again at the bodies. He still couldn't speak, although he was trying to. He tried to stand up. And after a few tottering moments spent refamiliarising himself with the basic skills, he lurched towards the bodies unsteadily.

He again tried to get to Marion but Amanda held him back. He looked at her desperately, and she shrugged and stood aside.

Chapter 33

Kate's phone buzzed and she prepared herself to receive the policeman. The door opened.

"Detective Inspector Flanagan, ma'am."

She looked up at a young, tall man with short, cropped dark hair. He wore a suit. DI Flanagan accepted the seat that she indicated and, without preliminaries, proceeded to business.

"I'm afraid I've some bad news for you, Miss Phillips," he said.

"Yes?"

"It's your secretary, Jane Pierce. I'm afraid she's dead." He looked at her closely.

She needed to find the right reply. She simply said, "Jane?"

He waited a moment before continuing, "Yes, I'm afraid there's no doubt. A climbing accident. She was found at the bottom of a cliff this morning."

Kate bowed her head a little. "This is shocking. Where was this, Inspector?"

"The Antrim coast." Flanagan produced a notebook from the inside of his well-cut jacket and went on. "This is all routine, of course, but I just need some background details. Can you tell me how long she worked here?"

"Just over a year. She started last January; I think." Kate screwed up her face, engaged in the act of confirmation and said, "Yes, January 9th."

"That's very precise," Flanigan said.

"Yes, it was the Monday after my last secretary got married. I was at her wedding, so I remember the date."

"Was she recommended to you or did she apply?"

"We use an agency for all such appointments, Inspector. When the vacancy arose, they sent round three or four people and I chose her."

"Was she good at her job?"

"Excellent."

He wrote all of this inconsequential information down carefully and said, "When did you last see her?"

"Well, we worked a bit late on Friday. Well after eight."

He was looking at her carefully and she could take no risks. She could have been seen leaving the building, getting in Jane's car or at her flat. A lie or omission was risky and unnecessary.

She added, "After work, I went over to her flat and we had some supper. I left her about ten."

"You knew her quite well, then?"

"No, not really. In fact, that was the first time I'd ever been over at her flat. Our working relationship was close, of course. It has to be. In her job she has, sorry, *had* access to a great deal of privileged and confidential information, and an executive secretary must have a good relationship with a managing director."

"Didn't she report for work yesterday?"

"No."

"Did she call in or was she on holiday?"

"Neither."

"Was it unusual for her to fail to appear without contacting the office?"

Again, Kate was careful. She said, "Yes, very unusual. I'm not certain that she had even had a day off sick before."

Flanagan persevered. "So, it was unusual for her?"

"Yes, a bit, but as far as I was concerned, she was a very intelligent, sensible and organised young woman and I expected her to turn up today with a perfectly reasonable explanation for her absence."

"Did you know she was a keen climber?"

"I think she might have mentioned it once or twice, but I really didn't know anything about her out of the office."

"So, you last saw her on Friday, when you left. As a matter of routine, can you tell me your movements since then?"

It was pretty tempting to ask why Flanagan needed this information, but Kate resisted this easily. "Saturday and Sunday at home all day. Yesterday, in here 7 a.m. to around 7 p.m. and then home alone. Today in since 7 a.m."

He finished scribbling down these details and replaced his notebook in his jacket. "Thanks, that's it. Sorry to bring you such bad news." He rose from the armchair.

She was conscious she hadn't asked him enough. A normal person with nothing to hide would probably want more details. "When did this happen, Inspector?"

He sat down again. "Some time at the weekend. We're not quite sure yet."

"And what about funerals and arrangements? Can I do anything?"

Flanagan looked at her keenly. "Do you know her family?"

"Well, no, I don't. As I said I really didn't know anything about her private life."

"Next of kin?"

"Don't know. We'll have a file somewhere. Do you want it?"

"Yes, that might be useful."

Kate picked up her desk phone and a few minutes later a woman arrived with a file.

Kate scanned it. "Not much in here, but you're welcome to it."

"Thanks."

She rose to escort him out. A final thought seemed to occur to him. "A dangerous business, climbing. I couldn't do it myself, no head for heights. You don't climb, do you, Miss Phillips?"

She shook her head. "No, Inspector, not my scene. Besides, I'm too old for that."

Chapter 34

Flanagan left the office and passed through the opulent interior of the building into a small car park. Each space was neatly marked with the title of its owner. He walked along the spaces and stopped before the one marked "Managing Director"

A car silently arrived behind him and he stood aside to let the endless German saloon park. A man in overalls jumped out. He ignored Flanagan and, with the engine still running, moved to the bonnet, opened it and poked about underneath.

On a whim, Flanagan looked inside the car. The interior was sumptuous and expensive.

"Oi, mate, what you doing?"

Flanagan could have flashed a warrant card but he didn't. "Oh sorry, just looking. Nice car."

"Yes, well above our paygrade, pal," the man retorted.

"What are you doing with the car?"

"Oh, I clean them every week and make sure they are filled up."

Flanagan nodded sadly and headed out of the car park. Then he stopped, took out his notebook and, before he forgot it, made a note.

He went to his own car but hesitated. The garage was just round the corner. He would walk.

When he entered the showroom, it was empty save for a disinterested salesman sitting behind a desk. It was an expensive facility, and not the type where you were instantly hit upon as soon as you crossed the threshold.

You either wanted one of these cars or you didn't, and you could either afford one of these cars or you couldn't. Flanagan satisfied only the former criterion, but he went through the motions by circling an expensive car purposefully. No one approached. He sat in the driver's seat, which finally drew an unconvinced salesman. "Can I help you, sir?"

Flanagan flashed his warrant card. "I need to speak to your service manager."

The salesman smiled; his judgement vindicated. He led Flanagan across the showroom until, at the far side, a small door indicated the service reception.

The service reception was unmanned, although from behind some concentrated shelving he could hear voices and a blaring radio. Despite the fact that he was observed several times by overall-clad workers, no one attended until, becoming slightly irritated, he banged his open hand on the desktop.

This action produced a man who regarded Flanagan with a suspicious and disinterested air.

"Detective Inspector Flanagan. I'm looking for the service manager."

"Aye, he's in today, but I'm not sure where he is."

"Well, I need to speak to him now, please."

The man shrugged and, without a word, shuffled back to the works area.

Flanagan waited and at last a likely individual, not in overalls like the others but in a passable suit, arrived. The new man had obviously been on more customer care programmes than his minion and smiled broadly, apologised for keeping Flanagan waiting and asked pleasantly how he could help.

"Is there somewhere more private?"

In answer, the manager emerged from behind the desk and led Flanagan back into the showroom area and into one of the vacant glass-fronted offices.

"I'd like to look over your service records for this vehicle." Flanagan flashed the registration number in his notebook. This request produced no questions and the man smiled, made his way out of the office and arrived back with a blue folder that he placed in front of Flanagan. "Anything else?"

"This car was in here last week. What for? It's a new car, less than a year old."

The manager was proud of his service. "We offer all our premier customers a complimentary check-up before the car is twelve months old." He reached for a document. "You see, a hundred-point check-up. It's just another example of our customer service commitment."

"Was there anything wrong with the car?"

The manager sniffed. "No, certainly not."

"Okay, let me have a quick look at this."

The manager left him alone and he went through the paperwork, although he was only interested in the mileage figures. The difference in the figures was over a hundred miles, and that was too high.

Flanagan located the manager. "When this car was in for servicing was it taken out for a drive? A road test or something?"

"Yes, a short one, a few miles only."

"You sure?"

The manager looked offended. "Of course, our staff are not in the habit of using customer cars."

"Okay, thanks." Flanagan left the showroom, considering his findings. What had he got? Nothing, really. Phillips had reacted fairly normally, a bit calm but she was a senior manager. Her answers seemed reasonable. But the car? It was more of a perk than a necessity. Three thousand miles in ten months, less than seventy miles a week, yet it had been serviced on Friday, returned to her on Saturday morning, and between then and when he had checked earlier put on nearly over a hundred miles.

Maybe there was a quite simple and reasonable explanation and she had forgotten something over the weekend. A family outing, a visit to a friend or relative.

Flanagan arrived at the office block, and after a nervous ascent in an unreliable lift, opened the door and entered his office.

There was a man in a black coat sitting behind Flanagan's desk, conducting a desultory review of the *Belfast Telegraph*. He made no move to alter his position on Flanagan's arrival.

Flanagan sat down and waited.

The man threw down the paper. "Detective Inspector Flanagan?"

"Yes, this is my office," Flanagan retorted testily.

"Colonel Pierce, MI5. I understand you are investigating the death of Jane Pierce?"

"Pierce?"

"My daughter."

Flanagan didn't know what to say.

Pierce moved on. "I understand you are the investigating officer?"

"Yes."

"Have you spoken to Kate Phillips?"

"Yes, I have. Are you interested in her?"

"Yes. Tell me about it."

Flanagan recounted his interview with Kate Phillips.

"Sounds reasonable," Pierce said.

"There was another thing." Flanagan told Pierce of his findings in relation to the mileage on her car.

"How far to the coast?" Pierce asked.

"Fifty miles."

"Interesting."

"Okay but so what?" Flanagan said. "I mean we've got an accident here. What reason would Kate Phillips have to kill anyone?"

Pierce pulled his feet from the desk and sat upright. "Inspector Flanagan, I said that Kate Phillips is of interest to us. Let me give you some background." He leant across the desk and produced a thick file.

Pierce returned to his newspaper and Flanagan read.

After about ten minutes Flanagan put the file down. "What now?"

"I have triggered a bank investigation, put some inspectors in. Let's turn up the heat. I want her tailed for a while, twenty-four hours a day. I'll arrange for a phone tap. Report to me daily."

With this directive, he rose and left Flanagan's office.

Chapter 35

Amanda was alternating between scanning the ground carefully and checking in on Jack, who was still cradling Marion's dead body. Whenever the police came it would be too soon for him.

A few minutes later she saw a green Land Rover emerge on the brow of the hill above the quarry. It proceeded slowly down the final section to the quarry floor, and after a bumpy ride, it pulled up alongside them. A moment later came Jack's 4x4, driven by Hamish.

From the Land Rover a uniformed policeman emerged while another sat in the driver's seat, engaged in a discussion with the in-car telecommunication.

Hamish and the constable approached Amanda.

Constable Kerr was about fifty and the right height and weight for a policeman. "Okay, who is everybody?"

Hamish made to answer but Amanda interjected. "I'm Amanda Barratt, Constable. Can I have a word in private?"

"Well, maybe in a while, Miss. I need to find out what's happened here. Firstly, we need to get him away from the body."

Amanda took a step backwards, beckoned the constable to join her and handed him a small card. Kerr delved into his top pocket, produced a cheap pair of glasses and looked at it carefully. He looked up slowly. "Is this part of an active operation?"

"It is now."

"So, what do you want to do?"

"Wait on the CID, and we'll take it from there."

"Who are the two bodies?" Kerr asked.

Amanda said, "James Murray, a local contractor, and Marion Stark. The man with her is Jack Edwards. They live in the house down the hill."

"The big house?"

"Yes, they just moved in a week or so ago."

"Are you a friend, Miss Barratt?"

"Yes, I was at university with Marion, and I've known Jack for years. I didn't know Murray – he's local."

From behind, another Land Rover arrived, and this time a man in plain clothes emerged. He strode confidently across to join the group

"Hello, Alan. What you got here?" He looked up. "Jeez, what you doing? Get that guy away from that body."

"Leave him alone," Amanda said.

The plain clothes man said, "Sorry, but this is a police matter. And you are?"

Amanda handed him a card.

He looked at her and stood up a little straighter. "DS Anderson, ma'am. DI Carter is on his way from Inverness with the SOCO team."

"How long?"

"Fifteen minutes."

DS Anderson returned to the group after venturing a look at both bodies. "When did this happen?"

Kerr said, "Hamish Brown – that's the guy standing over there –arrived at my house at 12 noon, and we arrived here at 12.14."

Adam Parish

"We found the bodies at 11.34," Amanda said.

"They've both been dead about two hours, I would say." Anderson looked around at the expanse of rough uplands and said to Amanda, "Are you sure there's no one still around?"

"I can't be sure. I've had a look around, and I didn't see anyone. I mean, would you hang about?"

Anderson said to Kerr, "First murder?"

"Just one murder in the thirty years I've been here. Liz McConnell, blew her husband's head off with a shotgun. Mind you, her husband was a bastard. January 1981, I think it was. Worst snow I ever saw." Kerr warmed to his recollections. "Still, we get our share of dead bodies here. Car accidents, hillwalkers, and plenty suicides."

"Can you get a statement from Brown?" Anderson asked.

Kerr ambled off to Hamish.

Anderson was left with Amanda. "Tell me about DI Carter," she said.

"Good man. He's local. From Inverness originally. Twenty years' experience. I think that's him now."

Amanda looked up. Three more vehicles were coming down the quarry road.

They parked and a couple of suits and a squad of white overalls arrived. A heavy-set man walked across. He spoke to Anderson, who went off to join his colleagues.

"DI Carter, ma'am."

Amanda shook his hand. "Nice to meet you, and sorry to pull rank like this."

Carter smiled. "No problem, always happy to help. Are your people coming?"

"No, that won't be necessary. Just do your job normally, but I need to know everything. Here's a card, it's got my number on it. Now I'm going to take Mr Edwards away from here. I'm not sure where. He may not want to be in the house, I don't know. I'll let you know."

"Have we got a statement from him?"

"No, I'll get that."

"Okay, ma'am."

"Right, keep your people away until I've got him in the car."

Amanda headed to Jack and sat beside him. The ground was hard and stony. She put her arm round his neck, and as she did, she touched Marion's dead hand. It was stone cold. "Jack, time to go."

He turned his face to her and said distractedly, "I know, but I don't want to."

"We have to. You need to get away from here."

"But I don't want to leave her. Where will they take her?"

Ordinarily it was an easy question, but Amanda swallowed hard and avoided it. With great deliberation, she detached Jack from Marion. She gave him a few seconds to get used to their separation then got up and tugged gently on his arm.

It seemed a long time but eventually he got up awkwardly and stood alongside her.

"You ready?"

He turned. "Not really but let's go."

Chapter 36

Amanda led Jack across the quarry floor and past a silent and respectful crowd then pushed him into the 4 x 4. Hamish was still talking to the police and said he could find his own way back.

Amanda turned the vehicle and drove carefully up the high road behind the quarry and then down to the house, a drive of about five minutes which felt a lot longer.

She halted the car and walked round to the passenger door and opened it. Jack was staring blankly ahead.

"Come on." She beckoned him towards her.

He was frozen in the seat.

"Come on, Jack."

"No, not here, not tonight."

"Where do you want to go?"

"Anywhere, just not here."

"Wait a minute. I'm going to lock up."

She jogged into the house and inspected a few rooms. A home until very recently, but now? She flicked off a few lights, left a few on and locked the outer doors.

When she returned to the car, he was in the same position staring ahead. She turned the car and drove out and took the Inverness road.

"Where are we going?" Jack asked.

"Wherever you want."

"But what about the police? Don't I have to talk to them or do something?"

"No, don't worry about that. I'll deal with the police."

Jack said anxiously. "They'll want to know things. Where we were, that sort of stuff?"

"Oh, I've told them all that. Forget about the police."

Dusk was falling, and for a few miles Amanda drove along the deserted road. She reached into her pocket and lit two cigarettes, passing one to Jack, which, after a moment, he accepted. He drew on it deeply several times and she sensed him relax his body back into the seat. He leant his head back further and drew again on the cigarette, more loudly this time, and she knew that he was going to talk. She wanted him to talk and turned her head towards him, catching his gaze and his bloodshot eyes.

This contact was enough to start him off. He said in a clear, controlled voice. "She was pregnant. Did you know?"

The car slowly came to halt, and she pulled into a rough layby. Amanda switched off the ignition and reached across and held his arm.

"When she told me yesterday, it was the happiest day of my life. I thought that I was the luckiest man alive. I really thought that I had got a second chance." He was faltering now and he paused for a long time.

The night had fallen outside, and the blackness was total. Jack continued with a steady voice. "I had it all worked out – me, her and …" This broke him. His head fell forward into his hands.

Lights from a car flashed past very close to them.

"We can't sit here," Amanda said. She kept hold of his forearm and he put his other hand on top of hers. In silence, they drove for an hour until they completed the journey to town.

The hotel was unappealing, a large and ugly concrete monstrosity built on the edge of the town. Despite this, its car park was full and when, after a longish wait in a queue, Amanda opened discussions with the man behind the reception desk, it became clear that the hotel was heavily patronised.

"I need two double rooms," she said.

"Hmm, I'm not sure. I think we're full. I'll check."

"If you don't mind."

After a short struggle with an uncooperative computer, he said, "Sorry, nothing for tonight."

"Surely you've something?" Amanda demanded.

"Nothing at all, madam," he replied, "Except, of course, our bridal suite. And that's £350 a night." He folded his arms, satisfied that they could not recover from this blow.

Amanda looked down, delved into her bag, and threw her gold American Express card onto the counter. "Good, we'll take it."

He held up the card and eyed it suspiciously. He tested it in a machine, and to his evident surprise the card passed his test. After some paperwork, he handed her a key. "First floor, last room at the end of the corridor, madam. Would you like me to show you?"

"No, we're fine, thanks. Where's the bar?"

The bar was mercifully free of patrons, home only to a cheerful-looking barman who whistled as he dried and cleaned a large group of glasses.

"Two bourbons, doubles."

The table where they sat was a bit wet and suspiciously sticky. She gave Jack his bourbon and it was finished before she sat down.

The Quartermaster

She went back to the bar and ordered two more, both of which she put in front of him.

Jack looked at her. "I thought I was meant to cut down on drinking."

She smiled sadly at him and sipped at the bitter whiskey.

The barman walked over. He elected not to wipe the table clean and said, "I'm just about to close. Would you care for another drink?"

Jack said, "We need a bottle of Jim Beam."

The man shook his head. "Sorry, sir, we can't sell alcohol by the bottle."

Jack delved into his pocket and counted out five twenty-pound notes. "Look, we're residents. Send the bottle to the bridal suite."

The barman picked up the notes and said, "Well, as it's a special occasion, we can make an exception." He leant forward, gave the table a light wiping and returned to the bar.

"You want to go to the room?" Amanda asked.

"Yes, I don't want to sit here."

In fairness to the hotel, the bridal suite wasn't anything like as tacky as Amanda had feared. And it was a suite, with three separate areas: a lounging area and a smaller bedroom off the main bedroom.

The bourbon, an ice bucket and two glasses were already delivered to the lounge, and they sat in opposite sofas either side of a glass table.

Jack immediately turned his attention to the bottle. Unhindered now by standard optic measures, he poured himself an outrageous amount. He looked at Amanda. She held up her hand. "No, I'm sticking to coffee."

She fixed it herself and, wandering into the bedroom, phoned Detective Inspector Carter.

When she finished, Jack was standing behind her. "What did he say?"

"Oh, nothing much."

"I need to know, come and sit down and tell me."

"You sure?"

He sighed. "Not really, but what else can I do?"

Amanda followed him through, and they sat down. Jack poured more bourbon. "Don't the police want to speak to me?"

"No, don't worry about that. I spoke to them."

"And they were happy?"

"Yes."

"That seems odd to me. Why would they listen to you?"

Amanda sipped her coffee. "Never mind about that. Just rest now. We can deal with everything later."

Chapter 37

After her late-night chat with Barras, Kate Phillips was more convinced than ever that maintaining her liberty was going to be a challenge. She was now working on the assumption that her mobile and house phone were being tapped, and there was every possibility that she was being tailed.

A period of inactivity seemed indicated, but that wasn't an option. She had to see McQueen, and she knew she would have to be careful. He would have to make ready to move – and as quickly as possible. He would complain about the timescales and berate those whom he considered responsible for the botch-up, but he would manage. He had to manage. It was the largest and most important consignment ever commissioned for their volunteers, and everything was now up to her and McQueen.

If they failed, they could lose the coming war in an afternoon. Compared with the difficulties Captain Crawford, that legendary old Ulster gunrunner, had overcome all those years ago, their task was a simple one. They couldn't fail now. They *wouldn't* fail now.

Adam Parish

When the British security services were interested in you, the simple act of arranging a meeting was suddenly difficult. But Belfast was *her* town.

She looked at the clock. Three in the afternoon. She pulled off a Post-it note and scribbled a time and place. She folded it before stapling it to a twenty-pound note, then folded the banknote in half and carefully slipped it into her pocket.

The hotel was only a five-minute walk, but she decided to take her car. Checking it for bugs in the car park would have to wait, so she looked around deliberately but saw nothing. She turned right a few times in a vague counter-surveillance effort but again noted nothing unusual.

The bar was crowded, which helped a bit. With an effort she made her way to the bar and struggled onto a stool, all the time keeping an eye on the door.

A barman pushed past another to serve her.

"Vodka and tonic," Kate said.

He returned with the drink and she handed him the twenty-pound note.

Kate watched him as he worked at the till. He was certainly smooth.

"Your change, madam."

She looked behind and to the bar door.

A well-built tall man in a suit was entering and scanning the room. She looked at him closely. She would see him again.

She waited until he decided on a course of action, heading through to a far end of the lounge bar. For a moment, he had his back to her. She had a sip of vodka and walked quickly out of the bar and was back at her desk in the office a few minutes later.

***

The digital clock in Kate's lounge didn't tick, but it still went achingly slowly, and Kate, sitting thumbing an uninteresting magazine, was anxious. It was quite a novel sensation. Never before had she had difficulty living her chaotic life. But tonight, it felt different. She tried the television and scanned many channels. How banal all the programmes seemed. She looked round the room. It was large and it was expensively furnished – a fair reward for her hard work. Would she miss it?

It was time to leave. She looked round the flat for perhaps the last time. It was just a flat. She flung on a coat and emerged into the night air.

It was already freezing with a thick fog descending, and with exaggerated care she wiped the windscreen clean, then gave the engine some loud and unnecessary revolutions before driving carefully out of the drive.

Almost immediately headlights were visible in her rear-view mirror at a constant distance behind. This didn't really matter. She had planned for this. She parked her car and approached the office door, waiting patiently for a slothful security guard to respond. His pace quickened and his posture improved when he recognised her. He pulled the door open. "Good evening, Miss Phillips."

"Hi, Jim. I'll be in for about an hour. Anyone else in?"

"No, ma'am, all quiet."

Her office looked unchanged – on second glance maybe a little tidier. Maybe they had been here. She removed her coat and flicked off her shoes. From inside her briefcase she took out a pair of training shoes, which, with an effort, she forced onto her feet. Having done this, she had a laugh at the sartorial effect of this change.

Then it was a ten-minute wait, but it seemed longer before her watch struggled round to nine. She locked the office and left by the back door. The fog had thickened, and as she looked right and left, there was nothing. She eased her way out of the building. She turned and pushed the door back not quite shut, stopped from blowing out by a large stone she had left there earlier.

Steeling herself against the cold of the night, she broke into a jog down the unlit alleyway until it met the main road. Breathing heavily, she looked left and right. All was clear.

Milligan's was a popular bar situated in what passed for neutral territory in Belfast. It was home to a throng of late-night city pleasure seekers: office clerks lingering after the day's work, theatregoers and cinemagoers, and a lot of men with long beards indulging their passion for real beer and jazz. It was always so busy that no one noticed anybody else, and – especially – no one noticed anyone else's footwear.

The jazz and the smell of alcohol hit her before she arrived at the saloon-style doors, and as she approached, she could hear that the bar was as busy as she had hoped that it would be.

As she pulled back the door and scanned the crowd, there was no sign of McQueen. He would be in the deepest recess. She struggled past group after group, excusing herself numerous times, until at the furthest end of the horseshoe bar she saw him.

She sidled up alongside. When a short, urgent meeting was required, McQueen was your man. He said little and gave and listened to only the essential facts.

She gave him the facts.

He scowled. "It just can't be done, Kate. Two days is the absolute minimum to arrange pick-up. And it'll take about a week before the units are ready."

"But if we have to uplift before the units are ready?"

He shrugged. "Split it up, in half a dozen lorries. Some farms maybe. I'll work out something."

"As fast as possible, then."

McQueen returned to his pint and said, "Aye fine."

Her return jog was uneventful, and nothing had been disturbed in the alley at the fire door. She re-entered, closed the doors firmly and made her way up the service stairs. There was nobody in the corridor as she emerged at the head of the stairs, and she moved quickly back into her office. She changed her shoes and, a moment later, was locking her office door for the final time. Before she entered the car, she was sure that she could make out the outline of the car still parked up the side road.

Chapter 38

Amanda had risked leaving Jack alone for an hour and had shopped for a few essentials. He had been drunk when she'd left him; however, when she returned, at least he wasn't drinking. But after listening to him stumbling over the simple sentence he employed in greeting her, she realised she was wrong and that he was still drunk.

If the police were on time, and they usually were, she had less than half an hour to get him into shape. She spied a three-quarter-full bottle of bourbon on the table, which might have been a second one, picked it up and poured it down the bathroom sink.

This stirred Jack into an incoherent protest, but he didn't have the energy to oppose her, and without much further complaint he turned his attention to the strong black coffee she placed in front of him.

At exactly seven o'clock the telephone rang and a detached voice advised her that the police had arrived.

"That's the police," she said. "Hopefully they'll have an update. You okay?"

"Yes."

There was a sharp knock at the door and Amanda rose and admitted Detectives Carter and Anderson.

The Quartermaster

They sat down and both accepted her offer of coffee.

Carter looked hard at Jack. "Are you okay to talk, Mr Edwards?"

"Yes, I want to know what's going on."

Carter said, "Firstly, can I just confirm the timings with you?"

Amanda wasn't that confident, but Jack responded concisely and confidently. "Murray arrived, and we, all three, headed up to the quarry. It took maybe fifteen minutes to get up to the quarry. We had a chat and after about ten minutes they started talking about contracts, so I headed back."

"You weren't concerned about contracts?"

"No, Marion was a lawyer to trade and was really leading the work."

He bowed his head and Amanda touched his arm and said quietly, "Okay?"

The sergeant interjected. "When exactly did you leave them, sir?"

Jack said, "I went down to the village, went to the shop, had a word with the local minister, and then Hamish picked me up and we returned to the house. Miss Barratt was there. That was about 11.15, roughly."

"And when you were walking in the village, sir, did you meet anyone?"

"Miss Crawford in her shop and Reverend McCallum at his house, that's all."

The sergeant responded to a break in Jack's voice. "Yes, I can understand that this is difficult, sir. How well did you know Murray?"

"Not very well," Jack said. "In fact, I only met him a few days ago."

The sergeant was nearly finished with Jack. "Tell me, sir, can you think of anyone or any reason why they might have been killed?"

Jack shook his head. "No. How can there be a reason?"

DI Carter then looked at Amanda.

"I got up late, about ten thirty and found that the house was empty so I just, well, lay around until Jack arrived back with Mr Brown."

Carter changed tack at this point and said to Amanda, "How long have you known Mr Edwards, Mrs Barratt?"

She considered. "About seven years."

"And how would you describe your relationship?" he continued, looking across the room to the four-poster bed.

She responded quickly. "Professional, and friendly, of course."

This was also noted without comment and the sergeant sat back, apparently out of prepared questions.

Jack, however, had a question and asked hopelessly, "Can you tell us anything?"

Carter said guardedly, "Well, there's not much to say at the moment, sir. Murray was killed by a blow to the temple. Maybe he was up some rocks. It could have been an accident. That's going to be difficult to determine. Miss Stark, well, shot twice."

Jack continued miserably, "But who would want to kill Marion?"

"No idea, sir. But it could have been anyone."

"Well, there has to be a reason, surely?"

"There always is, sir, but we just don't know it yet."

"What about forensic evidence?" Amanda asked.

Carter shook his head. "No report yet, ma'am."

"Off the record, what do you think?"

Carter leant forward. "As for motive, we've got nothing. Murray seems to have been a fairly uncontroversial man. Liked by everyone that we've spoken to."

"I liked him," Jack said.

The sergeant continued. "And, well, Miss Stark, as you say, she didn't know anyone, so it seems a lot more likely that Murray was the target. Maybe Miss Stark was killed just because she was there. And she was shot from behind." Carter added, "Also, we think the bodies might have been moved."

"How do you know that?" asked Jack.

"Both bodies have cuts and abrasions, Murray more than Miss Stark. Maybe they were dragged over rough ground. Who knows?"

"And Murray was dragged further?"

"Well, he was a lot heavier."

Jack had fallen silent, bemused and out of energy.

The policeman said, "Well, that's all for now, but it's quite likely we'll need to speak again. Do you intend to stay in this hotel?"

Amanda cast a quick glance at Jack and he shrugged.

They sat in silence for a little while after the police had departed.

"What do you want to do now?" Amanda asked.

Jack raised his head and summoned up a bit of determination. "I want to go home."

"When do you want to go?"

"Now. I can't stand any more of this hotel."

Amanda's mobile rang. She listened, as she always did when he spoke. As usual, he was succinct, sure and clear. The telephone was for a message and not a conversation and she contributed only the word "yes"

"Who's that?"

"Oh, just a friend." She was deep in thought. "I need to go out for a while."

Jack's face fell. "Will you be back soon?"

"I don't know. Maybe not. You could get a taxi back, or maybe Hamish can give you a lift?"

"I'd rather go with you," Jack said.

"Yes, but I have to go out. I'll call you."

"Later tonight?"

"Soon as I can."

She started to pick up a few things, which she put in her bag.

Jack picked up his phone, and a moment later he was through to Hamish. "Amanda's going away for the day, and she's taken the car. I want to go back home. Could you come and collect me and take me over?"

Brown sounded a little reluctant. "You sure? Why don't you give it another day? Isn't it better to keep your mind away off everything?"

"I don't want to take my mind off everything. I want to go home, but I can get a taxi if you're too busy."

Hamish, with a little reluctance, gave way. "All right, I'll come over, but I need an hour or so. I'll try and get over about ten. Okay?"

"As soon as you can. Thanks."

Amanda leant over and kissed Jack on the cheek. "See you later."

Chapter 39

One advantage of conducting surveillance in the Highlands of Scotland was the absence of alternative routes, and after a wait of about an hour, the car sped past the junction. It was going fast, and Amanda allowed it only a few seconds before she emerged from the viewpoint.

On the other hand, a disadvantage was that the scarcity of traffic made following without discovery a difficult business. At first the road was broad and smooth, winding its way through a flat plain of an extended valley. This enabled her to maintain a long distance between herself and the car, but as the road rose and then became an undulating single-track road, the distance had to be narrowed, and when the sleek black saloon stopped in a narrow layby, Amanda had to do the same, about half a mile behind. She would get away with this once, but not again. She consulted a road map. The road was a dead end. This was a complication. There were only a very few houses marked, and at the head of the loch and the end of the road, some six miles on, stood the Loch Tralloch Hotel, which a Google search established was a fairly large establishment.

She picked up her mobile. She was lucky: the signal was weak but steady. She had to shout and repeat herself but eventually was able to confirm a reservation. A prior reservation might give her some cover. Happy with the course of events, she lit a cigarette, put her feet up on the dash and looked out at the panorama. She sat for about half an hour before driving slowly down the road.

It was a long six-mile drive across mean and barren moorland, and as she drove along the route, she was continually looking for branches off the road. There were none, and all the properties indicated on the map were near the road, providing no cover for the large German saloon.

Out of nowhere, there appeared a luxuriant hedge, then banks of rhododendrons and finally a cultivated lawn. Then a signpost to the hotel.

The Loch Tralloch Hotel was a typical Victorian shooting lodge, and its cultured sandstone façade had worn very well. She parked in a large car park. There was no sign of the black saloon. The interior was in keeping with the exterior. The wood panelling looked original and the slight suggestion of dustiness only added to its Edwardian authenticity. Above her head was a full complement of stuffed animals and birds. Amanda hated places like this. She approached the main desk, accompanied by loud ticking from a grandfather clock to break the silence.

There was no one at the desk, but she didn't ring the little bell as a sign requested; instead, she leant over the counter, lifted the registration book and noted the previous entry.

She replaced the register just as a man appeared, and from his tone, she guessed that he might have seen her. He said, rather stiffly, "Can I help you, madam?"

"Yes. I booked earlier. Mrs Barratt."

He looked at her critically and, with a little difficulty, located the reservation, scribbled as an addendum to the day's diary.

"Yes, here it is," he said and emerged from behind the counter with a key. He said pompously, "Do you have luggage, Mrs Barratt?"

It was the second time today that she'd checked into an hotel without luggage and was getting used to it. "Oh, just a few things in the car. I can get them myself, er, later."

He led her through the corridor and up a staircase until they arrived at a small, modern annex well out of sympathy with the rest of the hotel. The room was clean enough but was modern and cheap, with fixtures typical of the ubiquitous modern travelling motels.

Served her right, looking like this.

The man wasn't that happy with the room either. "I hope this is in order. I'm afraid we're fully booked and this is our overflow wing. In fact, it's our last room."

Amanda pulled back a curtain, looked out over the back of the hotel and took in a view of a gravelled yard with rubbish bins and some rusting surplus kitchen equipment. It served as an overflow car park too, and it was full of cars, including an expensive black German saloon.

Amanda released the curtain. "Thanks, this room will be fine."

Chapter 40

Since he had telephoned Hamish, Jack had done nothing. He was restless and hung around in the foyer for at least half an hour before Brown entered the hotel, issuing effusive apologies for his tardiness. Without a word, Jack marched out of the hotel and straight into Brown's Volvo.

Thankfully, Hamish had left the dogs at home and Jack could enjoy a trouble-free journey. Brown never ran out of cigarettes and Jack took one from the top packet of three in the centre console.

"Sorry about the delay," Brown said, "but you caught me on one of the very few days when I had to do some real work."

"Disagreeable for you." Jack laughed mirthlessly.

"Yes."

As they drove on, Hamish was adopting a cautious policy in terms of conversation, which suited Jack. He eventually broke the silence by discussing details of his interview with the police. Hamish listened in silence and said, "Yes, pretty much the same as they said to me, although they didn't share their speculations with me."

"I can't get it straight, Hamish. I've been wracking my brains. I just can't think why. I mean about Murray. He seemed so harmless. I just can't imagine anyone wanting to murder him. You would have known him better than me. Am I missing something?"

"Well, there's not much to tell. I hardly knew him. I knew his father all right. In fact, he used to be a client of mine. He did sail a bit close to the wind at times, you know, tax stuff, and too friendly with some council officials, but nothing much really. Murray's is a medium-sized construction company, nothing special at all."

"What about business rivals?"

Hamish considered and said, "Competition perhaps, but rivals? Not really."

"I can't get the thing clear at all." Jack bowed his head to gather then order his thoughts. "You see, the way they were killed … So clinically and professionally, yet the killer or killers must have acted on very short notice. Why did they kill them there and then? In fact, the more I think about it, it seems so unnecessarily risky to do it in broad daylight. And how would they know that they would be there? I mean, in the quarry at that time. Did they disturb someone?"

"That's a lot of questions. I just have no idea."

"I think that it must have been important to do it quickly. And if so, why? And, of course, the police might be wrong. Maybe it wasn't Murray they were after. Could it be Marion? But who could have wanted to kill Marion? She hardly knew anyone. What could she have done in a week to drive someone to kill her?"

"What about Edinburgh?" Hamish asked.

"Well, she was a lawyer, corporate stuff, but she had been working less recently. Really just behind the scenes stuff. Nothing controversial, as far as I know." Jack thought for a moment. "Do lots of people around here have guns?"

"Yes, there can't be a farm without one, and there's stalking and hunting."

"Yes, but aren't we looking for a handgun?"

"I don't know," Hamish said. "Did the police say?"

"No, not really."

"Hardly anyone owns a handgun these days. Just the police and criminals."

This desultory conversation had achieved little but had taken up a good part of the journey. They were now very close to Mascar and about to come over the rise before the descent to the village. As Brown went over the rise, a vehicle crossed their path and into the quarry road. "Slow down a moment!" Jack yelled.

"What for?"

"That track leads to the quarry, doesn't it?

"Yes."

"Well, why would anyone be going there at night?"

"Courting couple?" Hamish suggested.

"Maybe. Let's go and see."

Hamish stopped the car. It was dark and the rain was hammering relentlessly against the car windscreen. He turned to Jack. "It's pitch-black. We'll not be able to see our hands in front of our face and it's a tricky road up there. Let's go for a drink at McAllister's or at the house. We can go up first thing, if you like."

This was the sensible option, but Jack wasn't interested in the sensible option. He wanted to go to the quarry. He knew that he wouldn't see anything. But he wanted to go. "Yes, I know all that, but please, just turn up the road. It'll only take a few minutes."

Hamish said firmly, "You're upset, I know, but there's no point. Let's go tomorrow."

"Look, if you won't take me, let me off here and I'll see you back at the house."

Brown sighed. "All right, but just for a minute."

He sighed loudly, still muttering, and turned into the quarry road. The suspension groaned as the first of the road's many potholes was encountered. The underside of the Volvo jarred as it grounded again, and Hamish slowed down to a crawl.

Now Jack felt guilty. "Sorry, I didn't know this road was so bad."

"I don't think it's been maintained in years," Hamish said. "Will we go back?"

"Fuck, we're here now. Just go a bit further."

The rain was harder now, incessant, and Brown cursed richly as he struggled to stay on what passed for a road. A moment later he stopped and said, "We can't go further than this. From here the road goes down sharply to the quarry and it's just too dangerous at night, especially in these conditions."

The car rocked back and forth when buffeted by the gale. Jack didn't argue this time. There was little point in attempting the last stage and killing them both in the process. "Okay, but just humour me. I want to get out. Just for a minute. I don't know why."

Chapter 41

Jack was out of the car. The storm was worse than it had seemed, and the casual clothes Amanda had bought him in town were no match for the driving rain. He closed his eyes and took short, deep breaths. The main beam of the Volvo allowed a visibility of a few yards. Beyond that, there was nothing. The tarmacked road was badly potholed and partly overgrown with grass and weeds. Jack inched a few paces forward, and then, in a moment of mental clarity, admitted that he had no idea what lay ahead. For all he knew a few false steps would take him over the cliff. He stood for a moment, surrounded by the storm. Although the quarry floor couldn't be far off, he could see nothing. The rain was bitingly cold. There was no reason for being here, nothing he could accomplish, but he had come and that was enough. It was time to go.

He made to turn but then he saw the car – or at least its lights. He screwed up his eyes and stared ahead, but in that moment, the light vanished and the blackness was back. He was seeing things now. He stood rigid, staring ahead. The lights came again, more powerful, nearer.

His heart quickened. He flung open the door excitedly. "Hamish, that car's moving about down there. Should we call the police or something?"

Hamish looked sceptical. "Don't be silly, the road's not sealed off – the police have finished. It's just kids." He sighed loudly. "Get back into the car. It's freezing."

"In a minute. You have a look and see and then we can go."

Hamish banged the steering wheel hard.

"Come on, a minute only."

Hamish swore again and got out of the car. "For God's sake, watch what you're doing. You're only a few yards from the cliff edge."

"You see the lights?"

"Yes, so what. It's a car."

"But what's it doing?" Jack asked.

"Maybe it's the police?"

Jack shook his head. "No, not at this time."

"Well, what now?"

"Wait a minute, let's see what's going on."

But Jack didn't have a minute. Through the gale an engine sounded, and before they could react the car was in front of them. They were blinded by headlights, coming towards them fast. The car slowed, but before either of them could react, the engine revved frantically, and the machine sped towards them.

Jack stood, still half blind and frozen. He regained his senses just before the intended impact and threw himself headfirst out of its path.

He landed heavily and the impact took his breath away. It was painful, but he didn't have time for that, and he forced himself onto his feet, chasing the escaping car.

The car wasn't going fast on the steep incline, but Jack was still losing ground. He knew that the Volvo was directly on the track and would check the escape, giving him a chance to overtake it. What he would do then, he hadn't worked out, but he powered on. He saw the brake lights come on as the car encountered the Volvo and it slowed and then stopped. Jack was gaining now, maybe twenty or thirty yards back. His lungs were bursting, but he drove his body on and was almost within touching distance when the driver made a decision.

The track wasn't great, but off-road was an almighty risk for any road car. As Jack reached out in vain, the car lurched off the road to the left side of the Volvo. It could have been brought to a jarring halt at any moment, but the driver's luck held; the manoeuvre succeeded and Jack fell forward over the bonnet of the Volvo and saw the rear lights disappear into the distance.

He cursed and looked back for Hamish. There was no sign of him. Jack lifted himself off the bonnet heavily. Everything hurt now. He began to walk back down the track. A little way outside the range of the headlights, there Hamish was, lying on the ground. As Jack neared, he heard him moaning.

He bent over him and cried with urgency, "Hurry, get up. We've got to get after them."

Hamish did not answer, but from the shake of his head and his grimace of pain, it was obvious, even to Jack, that he couldn't get up. "My right ankle's fucked."

Desperately, and with scant regard to any potential dangers of aggravating the injury or to Hamish's persistent howls, Jack hauled him up, and, with difficulty, dragged him the few yards to the car. Brown fell heavily on the car and raised his foot, his face contorted with pain.

Again, all was dark, and even Jack was forced to acknowledge pursuit was now hopeless.

Chapter 42

It was a long time until eight o'clock, and in spite of Amanda's best efforts it had proved impossible to obtain food. Aside from this setback, her task was proceeding well and the room, for all its disappointments, was comfortable, warm and, by way of a bonus, well placed to allow for a partial view of the car park through the iron fire escape that slithered down the outside wall.

Although it was dark outside, the car park was well lit, being illuminated evenly by four prominent spotlights. As she settled on the bed and looked up at the television, she finalised the positioning of her hand mirror. After a time, she had placed it such that, from her prone position, the car could be kept in view. She didn't expect it to move again tonight, but she watched it anyway.

As she looked at the snowy television, she became aware of an unpleasant smell in the room and glanced around in a desultory search. After failing to establish its source, she concluded that it came from her, which wasn't surprising. Sealed within the vehicle, the odours clung to her clothes, and she could smell the stale sweat and cigarettes now.

She reluctantly lifted herself off the bed and proceeded to the en-suite bathroom. It was small and modern and, although it had been fitted with a cost-effective and unappealing modern shower conversion, mercifully the bath had been retained. The water was hot and plentiful, and she drew the bath and filled it close to the top. After some fine-tuning, she submerged herself in the water. It felt good.

She wondered how Jack was faring in her absence and thought she should phone him. No answer.

The warm bath was heavenly as it soothed her aching limbs, yet she was uneasy about lingering. From the bath she had no sight of the car park and, after fighting a losing battle to convince herself she was missing nothing, she got out and, remembering the state of her clothes, flung them into the tub. She returned to the bedroom, and after a quick glance out of the window told her all was well, she resumed her position on top of the bed.

A second later the view in the mirror changed. A figure was approaching the car.

She slid off the bed and to the window where she watched and cursed as the woman opened the door and got into the driver's seat, alarmingly giving every appearance of preparing to depart. With her clothes wet, and in the bath, a sudden departure would prove awkward. The woman turned on the ignition. The car lights blazed but the car didn't move and Amanda, still staring rigidly, gave a sigh of relief when she saw that the woman was phoning.

She wanted to run to the bathroom and retrieve her clothes, but she didn't dare and kept watching. Her agonies were short-lived. The telephone conversation didn't last long, and the woman got out of the car and moved round to the boot. She emerged with a small holdall and Amanda now relaxed.

The woman stopped within the beam of a spotlight and began to examine the case, and the stark light allowed Amanda a better look at her quarry.

The Quartermaster

She was tall, maybe forty-five, and was dressed pretty much as any businesswoman of that age should be. She wasn't bad-looking but was coming to an age when she had to try hard. The woman concluded her examination of the bag, shut it firmly and turned and walked briskly back round, presumably to the hotel entrance. Amanda, relieved, turned from the window and fell back onto the bed.

It was nearly eight now, and she hoped that there would be no further excitement, so she returned to the bathroom, extracted her sodden garments from the tub, gave them a cursory hand wash and laid them on top of a warm air heater until they were passably dry.

In the deserted reception she looked for clues to the dining room. A waitress looked her up and down and grudgingly agreed to direct her. They passed several small rooms until they were finally faced by a tall, unmarked oak door, which the waitress opened.

Thus far, Amanda's focus on food had given her little time to consider things like dress codes, and her appearance in the dining room provided the existing diners with a momentary distraction. It was a handsome, old-fashioned room, tastefully lit, the walls covered with romanticised portraits of Highland scenes. It was small, home to about a dozen tables, all of which seemed to be occupied.

The diners were all dressed in appropriate evening wear, the men in standard evening dress with the females sporting a range of over-elaborate dresses, some garnished with jewellery. Some stared at Amanda, and she smiled back sweetly as she waited.

From through a swing door at the end of the room, the harassed figure of the man who had earlier directed her to the bedroom emerged. He glanced up and spotted her but continued past. He only returned when he had rid himself of some precariously balanced serving dishes.

He, at least, seemed to be too busy to care about her appearance and merely stroked his chin as he considered where he might sit her. There wasn't a free table, that much they could both see, and after a moment's pointless reconfirmation of this fact he said, in rather apologetic tones, "Would you mind sharing a table?"

"No."

The man turned and headed to the single occupant of a small table at the far end of the dining room. After a moment he beckoned Amanda across.

Amanda's initial difficulties on entering the dining room had served her well, so she was a model of poise when she sat down and introduced herself to the table's single occupant – the woman she had spent the whole day following.

Chapter 43

Hamish had been unable to resume driving, so Jack had conducted some tricky manoeuvring and driven back down the track and, eventually, to the main road. At the head of the track he halted and scanned left and right, but there was no sign of the fleeing car. Despite the closeness, Jack hadn't seen the registration, and all he could say about the car was that it was some kind of SUV.

He turned towards the village. "Did you catch the registration?"

"Sorry, no."

Jack was driving recklessly and there were a few hair-raising moments before he screeched to a halt outside McAllister's hotel.

Without switching off the ignition, he jumped out of the car and went through the main door. There was no one around, but he was not interested in formalities and moved behind the desk and straight into the small office. He picked up the telephone and, after a delay, was answered by a disinterested voice which requested he state the service he needed.

A moment later he was through to the police. The thick Highland brogue and the deliberate and structured requests for information would have calmed the most anxious of callers, but Jack got off to a bad start by first blurting out the events without setting the scene adequately and then becoming frustrated with the patient official when he reasonably requested that the story be started at the beginning.

Detectives Carter and Anderson were unavailable, although Jack was assured that his message would be passed to them. He still wasn't satisfied with the apparent lack of priority given to his story, but, realising further protestation might only lead to a still inferior service, he let the matter stand, slammed down the phone and swore.

As he did so, he turned and caught full the sharp and unwelcoming face of Mrs McAllister, who now stood in front of the desk. Her arms were folded, and she stared at Jack.

How much of his telephone conversation she might have heard he did not know, but he was uninterested in meeting her hostility in kind and said reasonably, "I'm sorry to have barged in like this, but …" He halted, and this time summarised matter-of-factly, "I was telephoning the police. Someone's just tried to kill me."

The words had a limited effect and she unfolded her arms and said nothing as he left the office and, without a further word to her, returned to the car. With some difficulty, he helped Hamish out and assisted him through to the hotel bar where, again, he met Mrs McAllister who was now, for once, working.

They made short work of the first of the double whiskies, and when the next was being lined up, Jack said to the inhospitable proprietrix, "Is your husband here?"

"No, he's gone out tonight."

Jack had more questions but bit his lip.

Hamish was ahead of him as usual. "Another?"

"No, let's get out of here."

The Quartermaster

Outside, the rain was torrential, and it was very cold. Jack drove up the cliff road to the house, but he wasn't wondering about how he might react to returning to the house for the first time since her death. Instead, he was wondering where McAllister was on such a night.

Chapter 44

It was after one in the morning when Amanda headed to her room. After the awkwardness of her entrance, the meal had passed pleasantly. The food was good, although perhaps not quite worthy of the wait nor the proprietor's boasts, and the company had been agreeable.

Very often when two strangers were forced to share a restaurant table the tension was tangible and the exchanges forced. But not so this time. Amanda had found her companion effusive and far from being hostile to the arrangement – superficially, at least, she seemed glad of the company. They had engaged in easy conversation throughout the meal and, on the conclusion of the liqueurs, they had been the last two in the dining room.

She had only had a couple of drinks but Amanda felt a little light-headed. Probably a reaction to a long day. She was very tired now, inexplicably tired, and she moved a little unsteadily about her bedroom. The bed beckoned her and she carelessly tore off her clothes and dropped them where she stood.

She fell into the bed and shut her eyes. The world started spinning. She suppressed a wave of nausea. She tried again, but each time she closed her eyes the room danced uncontrollably around in her mind. And then she must have slept. It might have been dehydration, or it might have been the spark from a car's ignition, but she woke with a start.

The luminous dial on the bedhead flashed 3.45 a.m.

She rose from the bed and stood a moment. She was dizzy. It took a while before her balance slowly restored, and she headed to the bathroom for a glass of water.

She cursed loudly on cracking her shin against the leg of the bed. Then the room became partially illuminated. The source of the light was outside, and she moved to the window, looking out in time to see the rear lights of the black saloon car as it drew out of the hotel car park.

She still felt odd, but the sight had unscrambled her senses and she began the urgent task of assembling her clothes from their varied resting places. She burst out of the room, still buttoning up her shirt, and flew along the short corridor and down the stairs to the reception. The reception was, understandably, empty. She had no time to wait and, grabbing a sheet of hotel paper and the pen from the register, scribbled her address and a very few words by way of explanation for her flight. This courtesy completed; she ran out to her car.

She pulled away, spraying an unlucky neighbouring vehicle with gravel. Even if she could overcome the ten-minute handicap, discreet tailing by motor vehicle was more difficult at this hour, especially so in such a place as this. The absence of other vehicles meant that no matter the distance behind, one's lights could be seen. Still, the lights worked both ways, and she thought that it might be possible for her to use only side lights and rely on her quarry's advanced tail-lights as a guide. This was fine in theory, but when taken with the bad roads and the need to recover the lost time with the consequent requirement for speed, it was a risky course.

Anyway, being spotted might not matter. She'd probably been suspected all along. What else could account for this untimely departure, or maybe her headache? If the woman had known then she must be very good.

It was true that she might have become aware over the course of their extended dinner date, but Amanda thought this unlikely. Why on earth shouldn't Amanda have travelled on the same road and checked into the same hotel? After all, it was the only road to the hotel and the place was packed. Others obviously patronised the place and could only arrive by this route.

She did not think either that she had inadvertently given herself away over dinner. Under her improvised cover as a marine biologist, albeit one who preferred not to discuss specialist aspects of the work, heading up to one of the many fish farms in the Highlands was surely plausible. Thereafter the conversation, although friendly and interesting, had been confined to largely neutral issues.

She kept the headlights on full at first to accustom her eyes to the light. She was far behind, and at the required speed, the drive was awkward. The steering seemed unusually light and the car was not handling corners as it should. She dismissed this thought. She was still half asleep and was driving fast, far too fast; the car was lurching and clinging to the road in response to her wrong lines around the corners.

It wasn't even the sharpest bend, but the car decided that it had had enough. The road turned to the right, but the car refused and instead continued along an easier and straighter line where only darkness and danger beckoned.

She stamped on the brakes and braced herself for an unpleasant impact. The snow poles weren't that wide and they weren't that strong, but the skid must have been slower than she imagined and the car must have hit it head on for, on impact, the car shuddered to a halt still, against the odds, on the road. It was true that the impact had shattered one of the passenger side windows, but this trade-off, had it been offered, she would have accepted.

The noise of the impact and the realisation that she had avoided a potentially greater calamity restored her senses, and she leapt out of the car to conduct a cursory inspection. The broken window was the only outwards sign of damage, and that wasn't important. The flat front left tyre, however, was, and she immediately realised that the sensation of lightness from the steering had been attributable to this.

How long it had been flat she could not be sure, but she guessed that it predated the start of her present journey. Pursuit was no longer an option; even if she could have located the spare, changed it and driven rapidly, she would have been over half an hour behind, and that was too much.

She climbed back into the cab and picked up her phone.

She gave him the facts without explanation or excuse. He loved her more than anybody else in the world, but this never got in the way of business. There was no rebuke, but he was cold and distant and issued several commands in reply and rang off.

It was at least twenty minutes to the nearest garage and there was nothing else for it. Being in no mood to attempt the wheel change herself in this cold, dark place, she drove Jack's injured car slowly along the road with only her failure for company.

Chapter 45

Hamish had wanted to return to Inverness the previous evening, but his ankle, which was now badly swollen, and Jack's desire for company at the house meant that he had stayed. The company helped Jack. He had not had the nerve to sleep in *their* room and had put a camp bed in his top-floor study for the night. It had served its purpose, and for the first time since her death, he slept.

They had been in the house for such a short time, but she had added some unmistakeable touches. As he came down the stairs, he stopped at the now dying flowers she had arranged on the hall table two days before. He turned for the kitchen, and as he entered, he looked up and half expected to see her welcoming and familiar form, maybe frying some bacon and eggs. She wasn't there, of course, and on examination neither were the bacon nor the eggs.

He sat at the table with a coffee and a couple of slices of burnt toast and thought. He really had no idea what he was going to do today. Or for the rest of his life, for that matter. The kitchen table was too big for him on his own and his thoughts returned to Marion. He would give anything for her to be there, sitting beside him. Not talking or doing anything in particular, but just there. He stopped himself and told himself to cut it out. She wasn't here, and that was that.

He thought it unlikely that Hamish would stir soon and decided that he must do something, anything, to get his mind off Marion. He needed food, but it was too early for Miss Crawford's shop to be open, and besides, he really wasn't that keen to face the locals at this point.

Sitting still wasn't possible either so he got up and went outside. The blast that greeted his arrival outside the front door nearly persuaded him to about-turn, but he resisted this temptation and, with his head down, strode purposefully forward.

He had a lot of time before the rest of the world woke up, and exploring the rest of the grounds seemed a good idea. He walked through a small copse of conifers and into an overgrown area. There was a suggestion of a track and he followed it. A few yards ahead everything cleared and he was very close to the unguarded cliff edge. He inched carefully to the edge and cast a gaze down. It was several hundred feet straight down to the angry ocean and some black sharp rocks. He moved back quickly, maybe thinking he might jump. A little further on there was a cottage, or at least the remains of a cottage – a single stone wall. He walked around the still visible footprint. It had been a fairly substantial structure once. He sat on a large stone and looked out to sea. It had a peaceful atmosphere, and Jack thought that whoever had finally given up the unequal struggle of living here must have done so with a heavy heart. It felt like a happy place. He got up and kicked a more recently deposited beer.

The night had gone and some of the strength of the wind with it, and it was now a bracing and robust morning. He walked back down the cliff road and stood again at the entrance to his house. He looked at his watch. It was after eight now and he calculated that, after a slow amble down to the village, he would not have long to wait for the shop opening.

He was about halfway down the road when the car pulled up outside the hotel and a figure that, judging by its general shape, appeared to be McAllister emerged, looked around and disappeared into the building.

For a publican he was an early riser, unless he was only now returning after his night out. A few minutes later Jack stood alongside the SUV and noticed that although the vehicle was undamaged, well above the rim of the wheels the vehicle was caked with dry mud. He frowned. It didn't mean anything, of course. It could have been any car.

But not the luxurious saloon which now sped past him. The driver didn't see him crouched behind McAllister's car, but as he passed, Jack slowly rose and wondered why his lawyer spent so much of his time in Mascar.

Chapter 46

Although not Wednesday, Miss Crawford's provisions seemed moderately fresh, and Jack bought about as much as he could comfortably carry up the road.

Their encounter had seemed awkward for Crawford, and throughout she had struggled to strike the right tone of condolence.

After the familiar struggle up the hill, he arrived at his front door and was greeted by Hamish who, dressed only in a shirt and a pair of shorts, had evidently been looking for him. When he saw him, he turned back to the house, and Jack noticed that, although he was still limping, it seemed a little less pronounced. This observation proved accurate, and Hamish said, "It's still sore, but the swelling's down."

Hamish led them both through to the kitchen, eagerly searched through the groceries and started to cook. The results were unappealing, however, and Jack turned down the burnt sausages and bacon, while Hamish ate enthusiastically.

Jack looked across at Hamish and thought that he looked tired. Behind the mass of beard his expression was as carefree as ever, but he looked worn and ragged. His injury and their adventures of the previous evening would be trying him.

Brown finished his meal, broke wind loudly, lit a cigarette and then leant back into the chair, expelling a satisfied sigh.

"Will you stay today?" Jack asked.

Hamish shook his head and said, "If you need me to, I can, but there's a couple of partners on holiday this week, and I promised them faithfully that I'd keep regular hours, at least for one week."

Jack would have preferred his company. With Amanda away goodness knew where, if Hamish left Jack would be alone. But he supposed he was going to have to get used to it and said, "No problem. I'll be fine. When do you have to go?"

Brown said sheepishly, "Well, really, as soon as possible." He looked down and lifted his armpit to his nose and recoiled from the sensation. "At least, as soon as I've had a shower. Maybe I could come over later, though? If you want?"

"I'll give you a ring."

Hamish headed upstairs, had a shower and returned to the kitchen. He slipped a cigarette into his mouth and hobbled to the door, combing his hair with his fingers, looking every inch the professional man.

When he had gone, Jack stood at the front door for a moment, steeling himself against a possible reaction on re-entering the house alone. It was as well that he did, because when he stood in the hall, alone, something triggered in him. For the first time he felt it. The first moment of the rest of his life.

He headed for the study and his books, but before he could reach the study, the telephone rang.

"DI Carter, Mr Edwards. I hear you had a bit of excitement last night?"

"Yes, someone tried to kill me, or at least run me off the road."

"Tell me the details."

Jack told him.

Carter was unimpressed. "Well, it's early yet, sir. However, I wouldn't get your hopes up. Without the make of car or registration it's going to be difficult. It's a big area. Besides, they were probably just curious locals, sir. And, of course, as far as I can gather no crime was committed."

"Hmm, they drove the car straight for me."

"Probably didn't see you and then panicked," Carter countered.

This ended the exchange of ideas and Jack hung up. Maybe Carter was right.

He made his way to the study. He found it as Marion had left it. A lump rose in his throat, but he forced it back down and, with a further effort, forced himself to sit behind the desk, where she had worked.

He had a notion to leave things alone, as a sort of temporary shrine, but Marion wouldn't have approved of that, and after a few more minutes the desk wasn't tidy. She'd have hated that. It was strewn with reports and paperwork relating to the quarry. It was a draft of an agreement which she had prepared in her neat and precise handwriting. An agreement between Mr Jack Edwards and the Murray Construction Company. It was short and precise. He read every word. When he finished, he placed it very carefully to the side.

He moved onto a thick collection of papers, full of numbers. They were arranged in annual order, showing monthly management accounting figures for the quarry operation. As he idly flicked over the pages, he saw that she had embarked on some kind of analysis, and ticks were present against nearly all of the entries.

Jack knew quite a bit about this sort of thing, but his mind was blank as he tuned the pages. He kept turning them; he had nothing else to do. There were a few crosses against entries also, and eventually he noted a pattern: they were all against payments to the Solutions Consultancy Group.

Why this should be so, he had no idea, but a faint degree of curiosity came across him, and he reached into a drawer and pulled out a selection of invoices and statements for the company. He reviewed month after month, each corresponding invoice short of detail, just with a total amount. At the bottom of each invoice there was an annotation. "Review!!"

He pushed the papers aside and again delved into the drawer. He pulled out every file but he didn't find what he was looking for. Not a single report or evidence of any work from the Solutions Consultancy Group. He switched on the computer and conducted a few searches. Nothing. He pushed the chair back from the desk. What did Marion want to review? At over twenty thousand a month, these services did not come cheaply. Maybe that was it?

From beneath the folder, the edge of the leather-bound desk diary protruded, and he pulled it towards him and scanned the days, to each of which was devoted a single sheet. It was open on the day of her death, and as he looked through the pages, he saw the clear entries for their meetings with Murray and hers with the McAllisters. And there was another entry. Jack had not known about this meeting, and he picked up the telephone. "Mr Sutherland, please."

Chapter 47

Above the wailing wind, Amanda thought that she could hear something from inside the house. The front door opened slowly and revealed a bleary-eyed man of about fifty, wearing ill-fitting jogging bottoms and nothing else. It wasn't much of a sight. Amanda said, "I've got a burst tyre."

The man yawned, open-mouthed like a hippo, and looked at his watch. Then he looked at Amanda. She waited. He was the only person in about a hundred miles who could help her and she needed him on board. She smiled at him, and after a moment he decided in her favour.

He lit a cigarette, reached for a heavy overcoat and moved outside cautiously. "Okay, let's see it."

She gave him the keys and vaguely pointed at the car.

Prudence and professionalism demanded a full inspection of the vehicle and he slowly circled it, aiming weary kicks at each of the tyres in turn. Eventually it was clear, even to him, which was the offending tyre, and after establishing that she had driven some way on it, and unnecessarily stating that this was bad for the wheel, he went through the small wicket door of the garage, eventually returning with a jack.

"You got a spare?"

"Oh, I'm not sure. It's not my car."

The man delved in the boot. "There's a run-flat, but that'll only do you for a few miles and you need to drive slowly."

"Can't the flat be fixed?"

The man sighed. "I'll try, but I'm not confident." He returned to the garage and Amanda moved to the light afforded by the still-open house door and looked at her mobile. The signal was strong. She rang but got no answer. She lit a cigarette.

***

The investigations into the source of the fault were taking a long time. She walked into the garage. The man was poring over the tyre on a bench. He eyed her suspiciously. "There's your trouble," he announced, holding up a small piece of metal.

She took a stride forward and examined the 9mm bullet.

He was waiting on her explanation.

"Can you repair the thing?"

The man thrust his hand forward. "You do know what that is?"

"Yes, do you?"

"Twenty years in the marines says I do."

Amanda laughed.

The man eyed her carefully. "Should I be calling the police?"

Amanda reached into her pocket and handed him a card.

The man braced himself. "Okay, ma'am. To answer your question, I can't fix it, but you're in luck – I've got a new tyre that will work. Give me ten minutes."

This time the man worked fast and she was ready to go in less than ten minutes.

She thanked him and paid him. She looked at her mobile. Still nothing. "Is there a hotel near here?"

"Yes, about five miles north, just off the main road."
"Thanks."
He looked her. "You be careful. Here's your bullet."

As promised, within five miles a large, modern, impersonal hotel came into view and she figured that it was good for a cup of coffee, even at this time in the morning.

Her guess proved accurate enough, and her arrival allowed the night porter the chance of his first action in hours. He happily agreed to produce coffee and a few ham sandwiches, which was good. Less good was the fact that he then insisted on sitting with her, but she didn't mind. She stared at her mobile. In the background, he was conducting an appraisal on Americans tourists who, although rude and demanding, could teach the British a thing or two about tipping.

She nodded dutifully. At last her phone rang.

He made no move away to allow her privacy, but it didn't matter. It was her father and she just had to listen.

"After you called, I got our people to alert the local police and we've just heard that she's been picked up. Heading north." He gave her the name of a village of which she had never heard, but her porter came in useful when she repeated it and strode off and returned with a map and indicated the location to her.

"I'm about an hour away, south. I'm on my way."

"Hurry. She's stopped at a local diner and the locals are keeping an eye on her."

"Right."

Unusually, there was a pause before he checked off. "We think it was her. We've placed her at the scene at the time. Nothing else yet. Nothing certain, but I think it's her. Amanda, so be careful."

He rang off and Amanda stared ahead, a cold anger rising. She had dined with her last evening and looked right into her eyes, and she hadn't felt it. Last night it was just a job, but it was personal now. She thanked the porter and, stuffing the last sandwich into her mouth, ran out of the hotel and headed north.

Chapter 48

Sutherland had taken his lead from the gravity and assuredness in Jack's voice and had agreed to drive over to Mascar without protest. The thing was now taking shape in Jack's brain and, as he pulled on a cigarette, he began to assemble the facts. Sutherland had been devastated when his preferred consortia had been overlooked in favour of Murray. Why? It could have been simple professional diligence, but as Jack recalled their conversations and remembered the look of desperation on Sutherland's face as he had left him, it seemed like it had been more than exaggerated concern for his client.

Sutherland had had control of Jack's aunt's affairs for a long time. He could do what he wanted. At the end, she would have signed anything.

Sutherland could have expected substantial commissions if the quarry contract had been awarded to either of the others. But not if it went to Murray.

He didn't actually know any of this, but it made sense. Maybe Sutherland was facing exposure from Marion and ruin because of Murray. And now they were both dead. Sutherland knew the area well; he knew the quarry and knew that Murray was starting work immediately. Where was Sutherland that day?

Maybe he could find out. He lifted the telephone, and in answer to a bland receptionist, put his hand over the receiver and announced himself as Mr Bain. He was terribly sorry, but he was writing to Mr Sutherland in regard to their recent meeting and he simply could not remember whether it had been on the 18th or the 19th. It could have gone wrong but it didn't, and the receptionist said, "I'm afraid I can't help you, sir. Mr Sutherland was out of the office with clients on both these dates, and when he is out of the office, he keeps his own diary."

Jack thanked her with assurances that another search of his own records would likely clear up the matter, and he hung up.

It didn't rule Sutherland out, but he had learned nothing really. He wasn't the police and didn't have to follow the rules, and he decided to follow up a vaguely forming idea.

A short walk took him to the village. Miss Crawford was at the shop door and turning the "Open" sign round to "Closed" when he arrived but evidently decided that she could give up some of her lunch hour in favour of him, opening the door and giving him a weak smile.

He didn't reciprocate. "I want to talk to you, Miss Crawford, about your friend, Mr Sutherland."

She stiffened a bit but held herself together and threw out a defiant response. "What are you talking about, Mr Edwards?"

In truth, he wasn't that sure. He softened his tone. "I need your help."

She opened the door and stood aside. "Go through."

The living area behind the counter was small and served as both a sitting and dining room. A large, crude wooden table was pressed against the near wall, and on either side of a smoky open fire were two low and tatty armchairs.

The table was covered in circulars from the various local groups in which Miss Crawford took an interest. On top, unopened and still inside its plastic wallet, a monthly marketing magazine was hilariously out of place. Perhaps the small discount that was on offer against a prominently and near-outdated stack of baked beans owed something to its advice.

"Will you sit down, Mr Edwards?"

"No, I'll stand."

"All right, what can I do for you?"

Some of the speech that Jack had rehearsed suddenly seemed flat and unconvincing so he said, "I want to talk about your lover, Mr Sutherland."

She looked at him poisonously for a moment, but she couldn't keep it up. Her head bowed a little, and she fell into an armchair. "No, not anymore."

Jack sat down in the opposite chair and waited.

"That's all over." She sniffed a few times but wasn't crying.

Jack said, "How about a coffee?"

She laughed weakly. "Why not?"

Beside the kettle there was only a single jar of coffee and two cups. He made two strong black mugs. She took it without a word and, with her head bowed, cupped its warmth with her hands.

Jack wasn't cut out for this. He said softly, "Look, I'm sorry, but I must have some information."

She looked up. "Is this anything to do with the murders?"

"I don't know, but it might be."

She looked at him hard. "What do you want to know?"

"I'm afraid that one of the police enquiries has revealed that Mr Sutherland has been appropriating money from my estate for some time and that, possibly, desperate and on the point of exposure, he became involved in the murders."

She issued a high-pitched laugh and looked skywards. "Money, fucking money!" Her eyes blazed. "Mr Edwards, you have no idea how I hate money." She sat forward a little. "I had fifteen years in the City. Every day listening to so-called colleagues about their promotions, their bonuses, their cars, their expense accounts. Nothing else mattered to them. Not health, not their children, not anything. They knew they had a lot, but they also knew it wasn't enough. And it could never be enough. All the time more, more. More to keep up with the neighbours, more to impress their so-called friends. And I … I joined in. Bought the whole dream."

It was quite a speech, and she wasn't finished. "For a woman, it's worse. Smiling back and saying it didn't matter when they accidentally rubbed up against me. Going along with their arse-pinching as if it was all a joke." The bitterness poured out now. "And then, one day, I just thought, fuck it. Fuck them all. And I got out and came here." She reflected sadly. "It was the happiest day of my life."

She laughed again. "At first, everything was fine but, after a while …" She stopped. "Well, it's pretty lonely up here for a young woman."

She didn't look all that young to him but he let that go, and she gushed on, "Then I met him. It was ideal. He was married and we could use each other for sex and there was no commitment. And then it started. Not much at first and" – she sneered – "definitely a one-off. Just a few thousand at first. Just until the end of the month. Then some more, then some more, until now. Until there was none left."

He felt sorry for her now. He said softly, "Is that when he left you?"

"Yes. You see, there was no need for him to stay. No need when there was no more money."

"Why did he need the money?"

She thought and, as if rebuking her own carelessness, said absentmindedly, "You know, I'm not sure. I never asked. I just wanted him to stay. I was so lonely." Her eyes blazed defiantly. "And now it's all gone, the money. So that's it."

She leant back in her chair and looked as if she was glad to be relieved of her savings in this way.

"Was he with you yesterday?" She looked up quizzically and he added, "The day of the shooting?"

"Yes, for a little while. When I told him that it was all over, he just went."

"When was that?"

"About ten or eleven."

"Can you tell me anything about the shooting?" Jack asked. "Has Mr Sutherland got a gun?"

She laughed, louder this time. "Him? If you'd seen him when I told him there was nothing left. He went as white as a sheet. He was scared. Not a man, just a pathetic cripple. He wouldn't have the balls."

"But has he a gun?"

"Oh, I don't know, but I don't think so."

"Did he ever talk to you about the quarry?"

"No, not specifically. Although recently he was fairly insistent, confident even, that he was going to secure a big deal."

"And yesterday?"

"Not good. Desperate, you might say. That's what brought things to a head."

Jack nodded. Sutherland was a strong man until you said "Boo" to him. Once you'd done that, he'd lick your boots for as long as you liked. Like all bullies, he was to be found at the throats of the weak and at the feet of the strong. Yet he could have killed them. He was desperate and he had been here on the day.

However, that was as far as it went, and it wasn't obvious how further progress could be made. There was, of course, the forthcoming interview with Sutherland, and when Jack thought about this pre-arrangement, it suddenly occurred to him that the meeting might prove dangerous. But he wasn't frightened by the thought of being alone in the house with Sutherland. And if he wasn't scared, either he and Miss Crawford were right or he was just plain stupid.

Chapter 49

On the walk up the cliff path after his interview with Miss Crawford, Jack's mind was racing, considering every possible approach to the interview ahead.

He poured himself a drink, went to the study and began slowly to tidy away the files and ledgers from the desk.

It couldn't have been long before Sutherland arrived, because Jack was still on his first drink when he heard the noise of an approaching car. He passed through the hall, anticipating the peal of the bell, and through a window watched as Sutherland pulled up.

He did not get out of the car immediately and spent a few minutes reading papers. This done, he emerged and gave his appearance a final check in the car window.

Jack wondered how it had been that Crawford had ever been attracted to him. He couldn't have been much more than five foot six and he was thin and weedy. When his premature grey hair and unattractive spectacles were added to the package, it didn't add up to much.

Jack opened the door assertively and discomfited Sutherland a little as he was caught adjusting his tie, but he recovered and entered, mumbling defiantly about inconvenience and cancelled appointments.

Jack made no reply to these opening pleasantries and, in silence, led him through to the study and took his seat behind the desk. He did not invite Sutherland to sit, but he did so anyway.

Jack looked at him. Although dwarfed by the leather armchair, he looked comfortable and at ease, engaged in a final examination of some documents within his small attaché case. After a moment, he appeared to be satisfied and placed the case at his feet, casting a thin and complacent smile in Jack's direction.

Jack reckoned that Sutherland might, at this stage, be able to withstand a full- frontal assault and so started gently. "Thank you for coming over at such short notice. I need urgent advice on the question of the quarry, now that it's, well, unlikely that Murray Construction will be able to take on the work."

Sutherland nodded sadly and mumbled some words of superficial condolence, and then went straight to business. "Yes, I thought that you might ask this, so I brought out some of the relevant papers." He reached down into the small attaché case and produced a couple of sheets stapled together and handed the document to Jack.

Jack overcame a sense of annoyance at this efficiency and glanced at the document. It was entitled "Peters versus Thompson" and went on to list the strengths and weaknesses of each party's bid. "So, you will see that there is much to recommend both bids, although, as I think I mentioned to you at our previous meetings, I would just opt for Thompson. As you will see, they're a solid bet – bags of experience and slightly the higher offer."

"So, two good bids," Jack agreed.

"Yes, I would say so."

Sutherland smiled complacently and looked at Jack expectantly.

Jack thought he looked too relaxed. If he was indifferent to which bid secured, no doubt they'd both pay him well.

"Do either of them use the Solutions Consultancy?"

Sutherland's face tightened a little, but he remained composed. He repeated, "The Solutions Consultancy," and furrowed his brow as if trying to recall an old and vague memory. Eventually he said, "No, nothing to do with either of them, but the name is vaguely familiar. I think we used them for a time in the old days."

Jack leant forward and continued. "From the records, it would seem that they were extensively employed, Mr Sutherland. Exactly what services did they provide?"

Sutherland delved into his case but retrieved nothing. "It was a good while ago, of course, but I seem to recall that they were a firm of explosives consultants. I think that they provided some technical consultancy when the quarry was shut down."

"It's funny, I've looked everywhere but there's nothing from them, just invoices. Surely there was something in writing. Some reports or something?"

Sutherland considered. "Well, they might not have. It may have been site work only or, if not, perhaps the reports have been lost."

It was starting to sound a bit weak, but Jack still didn't have enough information to press home the attack. He might not be able to bluff Sutherland into the truth, but he could put him on notice. He lit the fuse. "Yes, of course, that could be it, but I'd like you to look into the matter for me. I want to find out everything we can about the company. Their registered office – it's not noted on their invoices – their directors, company accounts, and I can't find any trace of them online."

Sutherland's smile was just holding up now. "Of course, I'd be happy to look into this for you. Mind you, it could be expensive and time-consuming and I'm not sure what the point is. Is it really worth the effort?"

"Yes, I think so. I've decided that it's important that I understand all aspects of the operation." He looked directly at Sutherland and added, "Of course, it was to have been Marion who would attend to these matters, but …"

"Yes, of course, this must be difficult for you."

Jack ignored this. "So, I'll leave this matter with you, but I'd be grateful if we could move fast. How long will it take you to report?"

Sutherland thought for a moment. "A week or so."

"Okay. Oh, by the way, who was it that employed the Solutions Consultancy anyway?"

Sutherland said, "I think that it was your aunt." He screwed up his face. "Yes. I'm sure they approached her direct."

Jack felt a frisson of anger at this abuse of his aunt's name, but he said nothing and continued to meet Sutherland's eyes directly.

Sutherland also appeared to have nothing left to say, save a parting shot, and he concluded with reference to what he considered the main business. "I'll leave you with that document and perhaps you can let me know which of the groups you favour and when you want them to get started."

Jack said, "Yes, I'll think it over, but I have a number of things to do. It might take a while."

Sutherland made to speak but checked himself. He rose from the depths of the armchair and looked at Jack. As he turned, Jack was watching carefully, and he saw what he had expected. Sutherland's face fell into an expression of sheer despondency. He had needed an early decision; he needed that money.

Jack decided to strike. "Sit down, Mr Sutherland! I'm not finished."

The Quartermaster

It was quite likely that Sutherland had never been spoken to in this way and the violence in the words shocked him visibly. He half fell back on to the armchair and looked up nervously at Jack. He made to protest, but no words came out. He slumped back into the chair; his body had given up.

Jack moved purposefully from behind his desk and stood facing and looking down on Sutherland, causing the lawyer to recoil as if fearing a physical attack.

For a moment, Jack didn't like himself, but then he thought about Marion and his anger blotted out everything. In icy tones, he said, "Mr Sutherland, you were in Mascar on the day – in fact, at about the time – that Marion and Mr Murray were killed. Can you tell me what you were doing here?"

Sutherland sat up and moved his head forward. He had recovered and he wore a defiant face. "I was in the area seeing some clients."

"Which clients?"

He blurted out a few random names. It could have been true, but the tremor in his normally assured voice made it unconvincing.

Jack said simply, "That's not true, Mr Sutherland. You were at Miss Crawford's shop in the morning. You went there to ask her for money."

Sutherland said sullenly, "That is none of your business, Mr Edwards."

"Maybe not," Jack admitted, but pressed on. "It wasn't the first time you had borrowed money from her, was it? In fact, from what I have learned, she's lent you more than a hundred thousand pounds in the last five months." Sutherland was disappearing now into the capacious armchair. Jack continued. "Now, it may be that there is a perfectly good reason for you requiring this money, and if there is, I want to know now."

Sutherland spluttered. "Look I'm not listening to any more of this."

"Sit down, Mr Sutherland! I'm not finished."

Sutherland disappeared further into the chair.

"Marion spoke to you a few days ago." Jack was guessing now, but he went on. "She asked you questions about the Solutions Consultancy. Probably suspected something wasn't right. She was a lawyer as well, did you know?"

"No," Sutherland said sullenly.

"Maybe she gave you time to repay the money, although God knows why."

Sutherland remembered he was a lawyer. "That's a serious allegation, Mr Edwards."

Jack said carelessly, "Yes, yes, it is. To be honest, I can't even prove it." He moved back behind the desk and lit a cigarette. He continued, "You couldn't get the money. Crawford had nothing left and there were no commissions coming from your friends in Peters or Thompson, so you had to do something or be ruined. There were two people between you and disaster. Did you kill them? Two birds with one stone."

Sutherland let out a squeal of anguish. "No, no!" Then he recovered a little. He leant forward. "Well, Mr Edwards. I recommend that you get a new lawyer."

Jack said, "Yes, that may be the best advice you've given me."

Sutherland laughed bitterly.

Jack looked at him with contempt. He was pathetic, just as Crawford had described. "I don't give a fuck about the money. I want the killer. So, Mr Sutherland, here's my offer, my only offer. Tell me everything you know, now, or I get an army of lawyers, forensic accountants, police all over these accounts. If I find anything, well, it's the end for you. If you talk to me, it's possible we can keep this between us."

Sutherland sighed heavily. Then he shut his eyes. Slowly, he looked up and, in a still trembling voice, said, "No, I didn't kill them. You can't think that?"

Jack didn't respond.

"Marion did telephone me. She questioned me pretty hard, and yes, I needed money. A series of bad investments – nothing dishonest, but I kept losing and I chased the money."

Jack said, "And client accounts."

Sutherland bowed his head. "A little. Not your aunt's, of course."

"Except Solutions Consultancy?"

Sutherland said, "They are a real company, or at least they were. A friend of mine. He is a mining engineer to trade, although the costs were inflated a little."

Sutherland looked pleadingly, but Jack was avoiding his gaze. He didn't feel anything for him.

"I didn't kill them. I would never do that. Besides, how could I have? Even with my glasses I'm half blind and I've never shot a gun in my life. Please believe me."

Jack said sharply, "A gun. How do you know that?"

Sutherland shrugged. "Everyone in Mascar knows."

That was probably true.

Sutherland returned to his own plight. "Look, please give me some time. I'll replace all the money, I promise. Just say you'll give me time. If this gets out, I'll be ruined. Please don't tell the police."

Jack supposed he should be sharing this information with the police, but not today. He was sure now that Sutherland was not involved in murder. The way that the man had crumbled in front of him was pretty convincing. As anticipated, a bully, trampling over the weak and fawning to the powerful.

Jack was a sensitive man – too soft, Marion sometimes had said. Sutherland was lucky that he wasn't dealing with her. She wouldn't have hesitated to expose him as a fraud. "Nothing worse than a corrupt lawyer," she used to say.

Her death had changed him, probably for ever, and all his weak and soft spots had been hardened. He cared nothing for the consequences for his former lawyer, Sutherland, but a deal was a deal.

"I'll think about it," Jack said. "Now get out of my fucking house."

Chapter 50

On the late winter afternoon, the Wild-West-style diner was deserted. Deserted apart from the bald man in the worn and gaudy pinstripe suit and the well-dressed businesswoman at the small table at the far corner. He was heartily eating a selection of unidentifiable fried items floating in a deep pool of grease while she, with more concern for her health, confined herself to a sour cup of coffee-flavoured water.

"I was surprised when you called," McQueen said. "You know you can trust me to get the job done."

"Yes, I can," Kate replied.

"So, why are you here?"

"Well, things are serious."

"I know, but they always are. Nothing else?"

Kate sighed. "I've got a few issues at home as well. I need to disappear for a while. Whatever happens, we've got to get this right."

McQueen looked at her. "Do you need me to do anything else?"

"No, just what you're doing. You're in no danger. I'll just tag along for a bit."

"All right."

"When are you going?"

"Tonight, at eight," he said and added, "and out of there by nine."

She nodded at this, rose from the table and, with no valedictory statement, walked out of the diner.

***

Forty-five minutes later, Amanda drove into the one-horse town, stopped and looked around the deserted car park. Before she could fix on her contact, there was a sudden rap at the car window and she lowered it.

"Constable Fraser, ma'am. Your target was here. She ate with a middle-aged man. They left about half an hour ago in separate cars, both heading north."

"Is anyone following?"

"No ma'am, but we have a couple of cars keeping an eye out at key junctions. They've got your number and they'll call you with updates."

"Thanks, Constable."

"Anything else, ma'am?"

"No, I need to go, thanks."

Amanda, with a fixed car and a clear purpose, screeched out of the diner. Tailing arrangements weren't great but there was no early way off this road. Besides which, this time she knew where Phillips was going. She drove fast, determined to close the gap.

Chapter 51

At about six, Jack heard a shout from the hall. "Hello, you there?"

"In the study."

Hamish walked in and went straight to the drinks tray, poured himself a generous glass and sat down opposite Jack.

Jack smiled. "Thanks for coming over. I appreciate it."

"No, problem. What have you been doing today?"

"Oh, just sorting out a bit of paperwork."

Hamish returned to the drinks tray. "Another?"

"Yes."

Hamish flopped onto the chair. He smiled at Jack through his untidy beard and said, "I thought about not coming over tonight. In fact, I tried to phone you to call off, but your phone doesn't seem to be working."

Jack got up and returned a moment later, confirming the fact that the line was, indeed, dead, but it didn't seem to matter and he poured them both another drink.

"Any details about the funerals?"

The question hurt Jack. He had banished this thought. "Amanda says it'll be at least a week before the bodies are released."

After a little time sitting in silence Hamish suggested, "Let's go for a drink. Down the pub."

"How's your ankle?"

"Much better, no problem getting to the pub."

When they stepped outside, the likely reason for the dud phoneline was not hard to work out, and they had to pull up their jackets to guard themselves against the gale and the hard-hitting rain. It was black, but it wasn't difficult to follow the general route of the cliff road, and it wasn't long before they were sitting in McAllister's bar.

Unsurprisingly, few others had taken the decision to venture outdoors, and the bar was home only to the ample form of McAllister, who was sitting on a bar stool playing the parts of both landlord and patron. The McRae brothers were in the corner with a lot of glasses, mostly empty, in front of them. Most surprisingly of all, the Reverend McCallum sat in the farthest corner, with a surprisingly full glass of what looked like whisky.

McAllister greeted their arrival half-heartedly, slowly producing drinks, and all three stood in a line, leaning against the bar, staring ahead. Several times Hamish attempted to kick-start a conversation, but no theme could be sustained and, one by one, they faded and silence returned.

Hamish shuffled off to the toilet, leaving Jack alone with McAllister. Jack didn't want to talk to McAllister. He was still wondering whether it was his car which had been up at the quarry, but he didn't ask. Sutherland might have folded in the face of his bluff, but McAllister would just tell him to fuck off.

Jack took a mouthful of bourbon. A moment later his heart sank as McCallum sidled up to him.

Good evening, Minister," Jack managed.

McCallum sat on a barstool. Solemnly he said, "If you want to talk to me about arrangements or indeed anything, please let me know."

Jack didn't want to talk to McCallum about anything.

The minister continued, "The church can provide comfort and support in difficult times."

Jack softened. This was no time for a theological schism. "Yes, thanks, I don't know what's to happen. I won't know for a little while."

"Well, let me know."

"Yes, thank you. I will."

McCallum turned on his heel, and Jack relaxed.

But McCallum had a parting shot. "What will happen to the quarry now?"

Jack, with a colossal effort, succeeded in repressing possibly the biggest wave of anger he had ever experienced. You couldn't punch a man who was twenty-five years your senior and a minister of the church, but you could be forgiven for considering it when asked a question of such insensitivity.

Jack's blood cooled rapidly, now stone cold, his brain sharp and alert. He looked around the bar. He started to talk in stumbling tones but he was having to work at that. "I-I don't think I could bear to open it now. Maybe I'll change my mind in time, but for now I just want to avoid the place."

"Very understandable," McCallum said and moved aside as Hamish returned to his stool.

Jack went on, "In fact, I'm going to close off the road and get all that machinery cleared. Give it back to nature. I've got a squad of people coming first thing tomorrow to seal it off and clear it."

McCallum listened to this in silence but for once appeared to have no opinion. He repeated, "Well, if you wish to discuss anything with me, don't hesitate."

Jack mumbled a thank you, which this time got rid of the tiresome cleric.

"Another drink?" Hamish asked.

Jack raised his hand. "Not for me. I've got a splitting headache. Do you mind if I call it a day? Suddenly I'm really tired."

Hamish shrugged. "No, of course not. Understandable. I'll have maybe one more."

"Yes, fine. Sorry to desert you."

Hamish was reassuring. "No problem."

"See you later. I'll call you tomorrow."

The wind had dropped, and the early evening sky was clear. Stars pierced the sky. Jack raised his collar and trudged off home, alone.

Chapter 52

Jack pulled the heavy storm door shut and, after a battle with some little-used bolts, shut it fast. He locked the inner door as well and threw off his coat.

He needed to work fast. First, he located a torch from the kitchen and then searched for something which might serve as a weapon. Thinking quickly, he returned to the alcove and located a walking stick with a leaded end. It was antique and crude, but it was better than nothing.

It was already cold outside and he might be in for a long wait. He sprinted up to the bedroom and put on several layers of clothing and a full balaclava, which he had no idea he had packed. Downstairs, he filled a small hip flask, put on his hiking boots, a head-torch and a heavy waxed jacket. He was ready.

Through the kitchen, at the far end of an old-fashioned pantry, there was a back entrance to the house. He turned the heavy key and went out into the night.

The first few hundred yards were easy; the ground was bathed in light from the house. He straddled the drystane dyke and onto the rough upland.

He flicked on his head-torch. Combined with a splash of natural moonlight it was good enough to guide him to the track up to the quarry, albeit after a couple of minor stumbles.

It was about a twenty-minute walk, but not tonight. Jack had wings, or at least adrenalin pumping through his system. The sandy, muddy track came to an end, and he was at the start of the quarry floor. Ahead, he could make out the outlines of the containers and huts. The going was tougher now, the carpet of stone irregular and jagged. The wind had disappeared now and the sound of every crunching stride echoed off the quarry wall. He arrived at the square collection of containers and stopped. He switched off the head-torch and stood still. He looked and listened. Not a sound and not a flicker of light.

So far so good.

If someone came, it would be by car, so he had some time and he would get some notice. Nevertheless, he needed to identify a place of concealment. He risked the head-torch again and the powerful hand-torch that he had packed. A short, cautious walk took him the length of the main quarry face and round past the outcrop where Murray had taken him. The rocks were dry and irregular, and with a small effort it was possible for Jack to wedge himself between a small fault that allowed a reasonable view of the quarry floor.

This done, he headed back to the containers and huts. They were all padlocked except for a single container. Jack steeled himself and looked inside. It was damp, smelled bad and was empty. He stepped out, and as he did so, a flash from his torch glinted against a small collection of tools. Jack knelt down and inspected them. This was a bonus. These bolt cutters would be able to handle the padlocks on the various units. Jack headed first to the huts. Both were also very sparsely furnished. In the first, a single chair and a crude tabletop with a few cups and a kettle, and the second a dirty and largely torn sofa with a tabloid newspaper.

The padlocks protecting the containers were bulkier but provided little resistance to the efficient bolt cutters. The first two containers were busier, packed with a miscellany of benign items, and Jack tired of them quickly.

The last one was superficially similar, although in the far corner there was a pile of tea chests. Jack battled his way past some old office furniture and created a space. He had time, so he pulled out the first of the chests and started to examine it. He pulled out some straw and then a packet of something. He shone the powerful torch on it. This, at last, was interesting.

Jack used his finger to count. He had emptied all the crates and had twelve wrapped packets of something or other. Jack wasn't an expert. On the television, you were meant to cut the packaging with a sharp knife, taste the contents and deliver a knowing nod of acknowledgement to colleagues. Jack didn't have a knife and he didn't have colleagues. He also didn't know what cocaine, or whatever it might be, tasted like anyway. It was one of his great weaknesses. For some reason, and despite half a lifetime in academia, he knew nothing about drugs. But he knew they *were* drugs, and with each packet about the size of a packet of sugar, Jack was fairly sure they represented a lot of money.

Someone would come for them. They tried yesterday, but they had been surprised. But they would be back.

He leant back against the container wall and lit a cigarette. After a couple of drags he thought that this was a stupid mistake, but with the tea chests disturbed and the padlocks cut off, one more clue to his visit could hardly make a difference. He decided he might as well finish the cigarette. But he didn't get to finish.

At first it was only a vague impression, then it became certain. The sound of a vehicle.

He leapt to his feet, his heart beating out of his chest.

He turned off the torch and the head-torch and left the container. He looked up above the quarry face. The car was near now. Jack headed back to his pre-selected place of concealment and waited.

Chapter 53

The car projected plenty of light, too strong to look directly at, and Jack was unable to get a good look at the vehicle as it crept slowly across the quarry floor. Worse, it came to a halt, as perhaps he could have predicted, at the entrance to the container and outside his line of sight.

The engine stopped. Jack listened intently. There were no voices, which suggested a single person. These deductions were fair enough, but Jack realised that now he had very little time. The drugs were going to take very little hauling and the car might be away in minutes. He had to get nearer.

He heard the container door opening and scraping against loose stones, and the sound of heavy footsteps on the wooden flooring rang through the night. He had to get nearer. His footsteps would be audible, he was sure – that was if someone was listening for footsteps. That seemed unlikely. Either way, he had to go, and go now.

He started off across the stones and to the side of the container. He stopped. His heart was still thumping. He ignored it. There was movement in the container. It sounded like the tea chests were being moved. If that were so then he could get to the container entrance and keep about twenty feet between himself and whoever was inside.

He inched along slowly, between the tight space between the container and the back of McAllister's car. At every step he listened for the reassuring sound of the tea chests moving. A leaf of the container door was ajar. Jack took a last deep breath, waited for the sound of tea chests and moved his head past the door.

Light was no longer a problem. The visitor was more familiar with the container than Jack had been, and a powered lamp was slung over a hook on the wall.

McAllister had his back to Jack and was finishing the job that Jack had started, adding similar packets to the pile from a tea chest that Jack had overlooked.

He placed one on a second pile and the two piles were now of equivalent size. He looked finished.

Jack pulled his head back. He stood on the broken padlock and his foot slipped. It wasn't much of a noise, but in the dead clear winter air it was deafening. Jack froze. The silence from inside the container was deafening also.

Someone was going to make the first move. Jack decided to.

He presented himself, framed in the opening of the container door.

McAllister was standing tall also. A lot taller and a lot bigger than Jack. "Mr Edwards," he said. "I thought you were feeling tired?"

"I feel better now, thanks for asking."

McAllister took a step forward.

"So, what brings you here?" Jack asked.

McAllister took another step forward. He flashed an expression of mock puzzlement from his features, which then hardened. "You got here before me, Mr Edwards. You know why I'm here. The question is, what happens now?"

McAllister was more than ten years older than Jack, but he was a bigger and more powerful man. He looked as if he had a lot more experience of this sort of thing. On the other hand, Jack was in the business of finding out who killed his lover, his friend ... the woman who was carrying his child. "I'll tell you exactly what's going to happen. You're going to tell me what the fuck you're doing here, and then you're going to try and convince me that you didn't kill Marion." Jack added, "You've got a few minutes before the police arrive."

McAllister smiled. It wasn't a nice smile. "The police? I doubt that, Mr Edwards."

"Suit yourself. Start talking."

McAllister was nearer now and his body tensed a little. "As I see things, it's you who needs to talk, Mr Edwards. You need to explain how I get out of here with my gear. And, of course, how I can be sure that nothing more will be said about this meeting."

Jack countered, "You've got a minute now. Talk."

McAllister looked away and he laughed. He moved forward and this time it wasn't to talk. If he had connected with the powerful right hand he aimed at Jack's forehead, it would have knocked him down. Jack hadn't prepared evasive action, but that didn't matter because a split second earlier he had made up his mind to strike the first blow. The heavy leaded stick smashed into McAllister's cheek. A beautiful stroke and a beautiful sound of fragmenting bone. McAllister was a strong man and he didn't fall down immediately. He reeled and staggered back a few steps, and in slow motion slumped to his knees. Whether Jack was legally entitled to hit him again was a moot point, but it didn't seem so to Jack right now. He moved towards McAllister with the stick poised.

McAllister looked up. His features were scrambled and blood was cascading down his face. Jack moved the stick forward, but then he stopped.

The gun in McAllister's hand looked like a Browning, maybe a 9mm, but that didn't really matter at the moment.

Jack stopped and moved a few steps back, while McAllister, with a herculean effort, got to his feet, all the time keeping Jack covered with the gun. "Well, Mr Edwards, this makes things a little easier."

He wiped the blood off his face with his forearm. "Now, Mr Edwards. Listen very carefully. We are going to change places. Throw the stick away."

Jack threw the stick to the floor.

"Now, keeping your back to that wall, move down to the end of the container. I'll be opposite and going the other way. Oh, and it goes without saying that I know how to use this."

A few tense seconds elapsed as they changed places, and McAllister stood at the door with Jack beside the packets of drugs.

McAllister issued some further instructions. "Right, now, slowly and one at a time gently throw these packets to me."

Jack did this very slowly. There were only about two dozen, and once this exercise was completed the end game seemed all too clear.

There were only two packets left when the sound of the vehicles came through the night. McAllister looked behind him and then to Jack. His face told Jack this was unplanned. The engine noises were louder now, definitely at least more than one vehicle.

"Sit down, Mr Edwards. And sit very still."

It was better than getting shot, so Jack did so while McAllister slowly pushed the container door shut. Mercifully, he didn't shut it fast, but it still felt claustrophobic to Jack. Outside, the engine noises became louder and then they suddenly ceased.

Jack got up and slowly made his way to the door. He didn't risk pushing it open. He could see nothing, but when he pressed his ear to the door, he could make out some noises.

The Quartermaster

Sounds of footsteps, voices, although he could make out no words, and then, a single voice, louder than before. His curiosity was powerful. Should he emerge and take his chances? It was a difficult decision, but a burst of automatic gunfire settled things and he rushed back to the end of the container and crouched behind the chests. It felt like a long time that he sat in this position, but it got easier after a while when it became more likely that whoever was outside had no idea he was here. Eventually he risked moving back to the door. More voices and more movement. And then an engine started, and then another. The vehicles started to move, slowly at first and then louder as the engines worked their way up the hill.

Jack waited. Five minutes elapsed and not a sound. He pushed the door. It stuck a little, but a rapid shoulder freed it and he slipped out into the darkness. After a few cautious steps away from the container and into the open area of the quarry floor, he risked the head-torch. It was a help but not enough of a help to stop him inexplicably falling on his face. He got his forearm out in front just in time and a jagged stone dug into his elbow. It stung with pain. He pulled off his coat and had a look. He moved the arm in various directions. Nothing was broken, but there was quite a lot of sticky blood.

Despite this injury, he was certainly in better shape than McAllister, over whose dead body Jack had tripped. Jack knelt and switched on the hand-torch. It looked like there were at least two bullets that had penetrated his chest through his now-torn leather jacket. Then there was the one, maybe more, that had caught him roughly where he used to have a left eye. Jack checked out McAllister's pockets for car keys, but there was nothing. He walked back to McAllister's car. He tried the door gingerly but it didn't yield.

He cursed. What had he learnt? That McAllister was supplementing his income by drug dealing. Yes, but he didn't really care about that, and he didn't really care that McAllister was dead. Had they taken the drugs? He walked slowly back to the body. There was nothing more he could do. He should phone the police. He took out his mobile. There was a signal. He dialled, and it rang.

A voice answered. He made to speak but he couldn't. From somewhere near came another low sound, then a slit of light cast itself onto the quarry floor. He put his phone back in his pocket and walked towards it. It was further away than he first thought and he had walked the entire length of the quarry face before he knew where he was going. He edged around the outcrop, close to where he had sat earlier.

There was more light now, a lot more. It seemed to come from inside the rock. A heavy-set man was standing smoking. He didn't see Jack at first. He couldn't possibly have expected to see him. He lit another cigarette. Two or three drags did the trick and he flicked the cigarette into the darkness. As he did so he turned slightly, and for a moment each man stared at the other's silhouetted form.

There was about two yards between them, and the man moved forward a short pace to investigate. Jack had done this before, and with every sensation heightened, he watched in slow motion as the man's hand darted into an inside pocket. He couldn't be sure what was in that pocket, but he wasn't waiting. He took a single stride forward and propelled his arm and leaded stick through the air, agonisingly slowly but quickly enough. Just as the gun came out into full view, the leaded end caught the man on the side of the head and he fell immediately limp onto the ground.

Jack was getting good with this stick. Maybe too good. He had never killed anyone before. He moved forward and was relieved when he knelt and felt that the man, though unconscious, was still breathing.

The Quartermaster

The gun had fallen from the man's hand when he had taken the blow, and despite Jack's stick ability, a gun would be better. It had started to rain and, kneeling on the stony ground, he searched around the body, groping frantically with both hands for a touch or sensation that would locate the weapon.

And then he felt it. But it wasn't against his hands.

The rain and the wind were cold, but the muzzle against his temple was colder. He looked up, dazzled by a torch beam. He put his hands over his eyes against the blinding light and the torch was withdrawn slightly, but the gun on his temple pressed harder against him. And then it withdrew, very slowly, and waggled in the direction of the rock.

A few steps on, Jack could see, there was a recess in the cliff.

He could not make out any details of the form that stood behind the torch, but the gun was waggling again. He was getting the hang of this code and he walked slowly to the recess with the gun occasionally pressed against his back.

He entered the recess and went through a metal door which led through to a small dimly lit area. He halted at the far wall and a voice said, "Sit down very slowly, please."

Jack sat on the floor and turned around. The small area was home to a storm lantern hanging above his head, but was otherwise claustrophobic and uninteresting. However, the figure that stood framed in the entrance and steadily trained the short machine pistol on him was more interesting.

Chapter 54

The figure was wrapped in a full-length waxed raincoat with its head covered in a similarly textured full hat.

Jack stared at the end of the machine pistol. It was held very still. This was bad. Only someone with experience of this sort of thing could convince a hand to be so steady. The voice was cold and professional.

"Who are you?"

He couldn't be surprised at anything after the last few days, and the Belfast accent didn't surprise him – but it being a woman did.

Jack was no hero, but he was wet and he was sick and tired. Sick and tired of folks on his land and of having guns pointed at him. Marion was gone, and at this moment he didn't care if he joined her. He shouted, "I'm Jack Edwards and I own this land and this fucking quarry. It should be me who's asking the questions."

The silence that followed this outburst gave him ample time to regret these cavalier – and potentially fatally mis-chosen – words. She moved a half step into the recess, now within the range of the light from the lamp, and sat down. Without altering the coverage of the machine pistol, she leant her head forward and with one hand tugged off her scarf, pulled off her hat and, shaking her hair in celebration of its release, looked at him.

He could see her well now – a well-preserved woman of about forty-five. Despite the clamping action of the hat on her hair, it was full and attractive. She would even have, in normal circumstances, been attractive but, although her face wore no obvious expression, there was a weariness to its overall effect which had put years on her.

She still did not speak but he, after his initial outburst, now felt weak and beaten. He fought this hard. He must try, by any means, to keep her talking.

He chilled as he suddenly considered the consequences of her decision to abandon her cover and give him full access to her face and features.

It was impossible not to regret his rashness in acting alone. Trapped at the dead end of a narrow room and covered with a weapon that delivered its deadly ammunition at many hundreds of rounds per minute was a bad place to start. He had few other options. There was no possibility of rushing her. Although she sat a little closer to him, she remained well outside a range that would give him a sporting chance. He could talk or he could die. So, he talked. "I've told you my name. Might I know yours?"

In the situation this formal request proved to be a surprising success and she said simply, "I'm Katherine Phillips. I'm from Belfast."

This much he had guessed and it wasn't comforting. People from Belfast with guns in their hands were usually to be taken seriously.

He feared that he would say the wrong thing, but what was the right or the wrong thing to say to a psychopath with a machine gun? But this was all academic. Jack knew that she had to kill him. Whatever she had come for was so important that at least three people, one of whom he had loved, had been killed. If they could do this, there seemed little chance that she could stop before silencing him.

He had a guess. "IRA?"

She raised her head and looked hard at him, then broke into a dangerous laugh and said firmly, "No, not IRA. It's not just the IRA that is fighting a war in Northern Ireland. The Ulster Loyalist Force, for and on behalf of the Protestant people of Northern Ireland." She said it with pride and Jack knew that he was doomed.

As a history don, albeit a mediocre one, he stood at a fractional advantage over nearly any other unfortunate in such a situation. Maybe someone so driven could be provoked into argument. He decided to give it a go.

He opted for a shallow and argumentative start. "Well, you're all the same to me, IRA, UVF, ULF, all relics, killing people for a cause that nobody else believes in, a cause that died years ago. Besides, I thought you were all at peace nowadays."

She looked at him hard and seemed to be considering whether this bravado merited a reply. As he felt a cold bead of sweat forming above his brow, she said softly, "There are thousands that believe in my cause, Mr Edwards, although it may seem old-fashioned and ridiculous to you." She paused again, delved into her pocket and produced cigarettes. She lit two and threw one to him; it landed a little in front of him and, after catching her eye and receiving her permission, he leaned slowly forward and picked it up.

She drew deeply on her cigarette. "Yes, I suppose it would seem old-fashioned to you. Unimportant too, I daresay. I imagine you think that we should concern ourselves with such important things such as the price of food and the weather and whether the government will cut our taxes at the Budget."

He was about to die but, ridiculously, he was listening to her argument. She wasn't a psychopath, and she seemed very, very tired.

She added wistfully, "Yes, I and our people would like to concentrate on these things but, you see, we can't. How can we when we're the world's outcasts?"

His spirits sagged when, for the first time, a note of anger and bitterness crept into her voice and she said accusingly, "Oh, it's all right for you. You're British, or you're English or whatever, you never need to question it. You take it for granted. You don't hear every day that the country to which you're loyal rejects you. You don't have that here, Mr Edwards, and so you can't know what it feels like. Ulster folk are as British as you. We've been there for centuries and we've never been anything but British. Never." Her eyes flashed defiantly. "And we'll never be anything but British. It's not complicated. It's really very simple."

This last remark sounded fearfully like her closing remarks, so he leapt in with an urgent supplementary question. "Yes, but what's that got to do with me? What are you doing here?"

"The other side are arming themselves. They'll be ready when the peace breaks. It's easy for them. Money from America, safe dumps in the Republic. But what can we do? Our people need to be defended. I'm afraid it was necessary to take temporary advantage of your storage facilities."

Jack forgot his becalming strategy and shouted, "And kill Marion and Mr Murray?"

She didn't attempt to fake an expression of regret. It had been done, and, if necessary, she would have ordered it again. "Our people need to be defended when the war comes. I couldn't take the chance of you discovering our arms."

With this sentence, she rose. Jack looked at her. He looked straight at her and, although he now expected to die, he wanted to face his nemesis.

However, she instead moved back out of the entrance and he saw her flash a torch. She returned and, the debate concluded, rasped out an order. "Right, get on your feet. And be very careful, Mr Edwards."

He did so and followed her outside. She stopped beside her prone colleague and made a cursory examination. "He's still alive, although you hit him very hard, Mr Edwards. Perhaps you would be good enough to lift him over to my car. This way."

Jack hadn't seen a car when he emerged from the container, which was good. He hoped it was a long way away.

Nonetheless, this would be the final act. Once the body of her associate was safely in the car, she would have no further use for him. Slowly and affecting as much difficulty as he could in executing the task, he painfully raised the man's body and awkwardly threw it over his shoulder. Again, exaggerating the strain this task was imposing on him, he shuffled irregularly across the damp and rocky quarry floor, with her flashing the torch ahead.

Eventually he saw the car at the bottom of the road. He figured it was still at least fifty yards away. This was a long way when transporting a man whom he estimated to be no less than two hundred pounds, but not far enough. He continually stopped to rest and took great gulps of air before, each time, the gun butt encouraged him to resume his task.

All the time he tried to close the gap between him and her. If he could get closer to her, it would give him a chance – not a good one, but a chance nevertheless – to rush and overpower her. Maybe she would stumble on the irregular ground. Whatever happened, he wasn't going to stand meekly and be shot. He would go out like a man. He owed Marion that much.

But she was too good for that. At no time during the five or so minutes did he manage to narrow the distance between them, and he felt like a chained dog frustrated by a baiting child or cat just out of reach, like in those cartoons. She didn't stumble either.

And still no glimmer of an opportunity had presented itself by the time he had reached the car.

She stood stock still, about three yards away. She came a pace nearer to give out her final orders, the last few sentences he would ever hear and understand. "Put him down, Mr Edwards. Open the car door. Carefully, very carefully, put him into the car and shut the door. Now turn round."

Chapter 55

He did as he was told and stood and watched as she smoothly raised the machine pistol. There was to be no glorious reprieve, not even a heroic failure. Nothing. He tried hard to stop his eyes shutting but he didn't succeed. Then the explosion rang out, its noise overpowering the quiet of the night. At first a single shot only, followed by a spectacular cascade of sound. He opened his eyes in time to see the illumination created in the sky by the machine pistol as it discharged on impact with the ground.

In front of him, Katherine Phillips was on her back. As he approached and picked up her fallen torch, he saw that she was not dead and her face was twitching and contorting involuntarily.

She might not be dead, but the fast-expanding red pattern over the chest of her pullover suggested that she soon might be. She could still move her lips, and he bent towards her but could not make out what she was saying. Jack was shaking now. He stared at Phillips and did not hear the approach of the other until he was tapped on the shoulder, whereupon he gave a violent start.

He had not expected to see Amanda, but she was as good as anyone. She didn't acknowledge him. "Get out of the way."

He moved aside.

She moved towards Phillips and looked her over.

"What the fuck are you doing here? And where did you get that gun?"

Amanda didn't answer. She was still staring at Phillips.

"I think she's still alive."

"Yes." Amanda moved forward and leant over Phillips, who was lying calmly with an occasional low moan. Then Phillips stretched out a hand. As far as Jack could see there was nothing to reach for, but Amanda didn't bother with much analysis. She placed the end of her gun against Phillips' face and shot her.

Phillips was certainly dead now, and Amanda bent her head a little nearer and said softly, "That's for my sister."

Chapter 56

This violent denouement occasioned in Jack a bout of severe and uncontrollable shaking, but Amanda was calm and unemotional. He had never seen her like that.

"Come here," she said.

He moved a pace forward and fell into her and held her very close. He was crying without tears and holding on tight. Eventually he said, "What's going on?"

She put her lips against his ear and explained, "I've been tailing her two days. Since she and her cronies arrived in Scotland."

"Why were you following her?"

"It's a long story. No more questions now."

But *she* had questions, after she had jogged along and back from the quarry floor. "Whose is that body?"

"McAllister, he owned the hotel."

"The one Marion had a row with?"

"Yes."

"What's he doing here?"

"He was picking up drugs, and he met Phillips."

"She killed him?"

"Well, I was inside a container at the time. There was a burst of fire."

Amanda said, "Yes, looks like a burst of 9mm. An Uzi machine pistol."

"How do you know so much about guns?" Jack asked.

"Never mind that."

She walked over to Phillip's car and opened the rear door. She looked into the back seat and re-emerged, apparently satisfied. "He's still out cold. He'll probably be out for ages, but, there again, one can't be sure. Wait here a moment. I'll bring the car down here." She delved into her coat and produced another handgun. "The safety is off. Keep an eye on him. Shoot him if you need to."

With this routine instruction, she turned and ran away from him, and he felt suddenly very scared. Only a minute or so elapsed before he saw the lights from a car slowly coming down the last few yards of the top road.

She emerged. "Are you strong enough to drive the car down to the house?"

In the circumstances it wasn't much to ask of the male lead. Without confidence, he said he was.

"Good, well, drive down to the house. I need to wait here for the police. I'll wait here with him in the car."

Jack said heroically, "I can't leave you here on your own."

She laughed. "Get in the car, I'll be down soon."

Jack came clean. "Can't you come with me?"

"No, I've got to do a few things and talk to the police. They'll be here in ten minutes or so."

Jack persisted. "But how will you get to the house?"

"Look, just go home. Pour a drink, one for me as well, and I'll be down soon."

Jack was very tired and did as he was told.

He pulled away slowly and made for the head of the road to the house. It wasn't just the fear that was making him shiver, and his uncontrollably chattering teeth reminded him that he was wet through and bitterly cold. Amanda had obviously been driving the car for some time, and it did not seem that it had even had time to cool down as the blower, when turned on, bellowed out an abundance of stuffy, warm air.

Her long presence in the car and the heater made for a heady cocktail of smells – not unpleasant, just the smells of a woman. And then he choked as the dry mixture caught the back of his throat as the stale sweat from his own body joined in. But the perfume and the smell of her was the dominant effect. It was a familiar smell.

Jack suddenly wasn't tired. He had so many questions. He thought about driving back, but he trusted Amanda.

He still wasn't sure why she had been after Phillips for two days. This was after Marion's death. But was Phillips in Scotland when Marion was killed?

He parked in his driveway. The Volvo was still there. Well, the pub was still open. The car was unlocked and he opened the door and looked inside. Things weren't unclear any more. Just some reasons were obscure now.

He went to the house, put on the lights and marched straight into the den. He poured a very large whisky, lifted the bottle and returned outside.

The moon was full and the clouds had disappeared. It was cold, but Jack wasn't. He went through the copse and along the trail to the ruined cottage.

The ocean was calm now, blues and greens with strips of moonlight, soothing and relaxing. He poured another whisky.

It was funny really. Funny that the full weight of modern science and police methods could not establish what to him, now, was so obvious. Just a little thing. A smell that shouldn't have been there. A smell that was out of place. Once that was clear the rest was easy.

Chapter 57

A gull late for its roost screeched and Jack started. Then, from a long way away he heard the unmistakeable sound of footsteps on gravel.

He shouted, "Hamish!"

The footsteps neared. "Jack?"

"Hello."

Hamish stood alongside. "What you doing here? I thought you had turned in?"

Jack laughed. "Not exactly."

He looked Jack over quickly, then said anxiously, "Are you all right? What happened?"

"Well, it's a long story, but here's some highlights. I've been up at the quarry. I've had a gun pointed at me twice. Oh, and McAllister's dead."

Hamish moved a step and the moonlight shone on his face. He looked anguished. "McAllister? What the fuck has he got to do with anything?"

"Seems he was doing a bit of drug dealing. Anyway, it seems he ran up against some more dangerous folk. Gunrunners who didn't take too kindly to him wandering about with a gun."

Hamish picked up the bottle of whisky and took a long slug. He said slowly, "So, that's it. They killed Marion and Murray."

Jack said, "Yes, I think so."

"Are the police there?"

"Yes, I think it's all over, up there."

"Well, that's something at least."

Jack took a mouthful of whisky. "Well, not quite over. There had to be someone local."

"McAllister?"

Jack looked at Hamish. "No, someone else. Someone that moved the bodies. Someone whose car had the smell of Marion's perfume. It was strong that perfume. Stronger even than dogs and cigarettes."

Hamish looked at him sadly. "How long have you known?"

Jack said coldly, "Not long, not long at all."

Hamish went for the whisky bottle again and then sat on the ground opposite.

"Why?" Jack asked.

Hamish was staring straight at him as he spoke. Like Kate Phillips, he did not apologise to Jack. It wouldn't have been sincere, and it couldn't and wouldn't ever be accepted.

"If only you hadn't given that contract to Murray. We only needed to keep the guns here for another few weeks. But, of course, Murray, with all his boyish enthusiasm, started straight away. I found him up there."

Jack wanted everything now. "You killed him?"

"It was partly an accident, but I would have killed him anyway. He had discovered the guns."

Jack nodded at this cold, perverse logic. "And Marion?"

Hamish stared straight at Jack but said nothing.

Jack had already encountered one fanatic tonight and Hamish's line was identical. People weren't important, not if they got in the way of the other's cause.

They sat in the moonlight in silence a few yards apart.

"Is that Amanda's car in the drive?" Hamish asked.

"Yes."

"Funny girl, Amanda. I've never seen a publisher take so much control at a murder scene. Is she in the house?"

Jack said, "No, she's still up at the quarry. She'll be down later."

The expression on Hamish's face changed a little, as Jack knew it would.

They finalised this short and logical mental sequence at about the same time. Hamish said, "Well, Jack, what now?"

"Well, that's up to you, Hamish."

"I guess it is."

Hamish pulled his coat back a little in the manor of an old-fashioned gun slinger, but Jack wasn't in the mood for nobility. He didn't give Brown a chance. After all, what chance had he given Marion and Murray?

It was lucky Jack didn't know how to put the safety on the gun Amanda had given him. He had never fired a gun before, but Brown was facing him a yard and a half away. Besides, it was Amanda's gun, and he knew it would work.

He was calm and his hand was steady. Two shots crashed into Brown, high up in his chest, somewhere close to what folks called the kill zone. He fell back but he wasn't dead.

Jack got to his feet and moved to him.

The moon came out fully from behind a single cloud. The cliff edge was inches behind Brown's body. He looked up and said something but Jack couldn't understand. Then he tried to get up. The decline in the grassy cliff edge wasn't severe, but it exerted more force than a man with two bullets in him could resist. In slow motion, but noiselessly, Brown, with a benign expression, rolled over the cliff.

Chapter 58

Jack couldn't be sure whether it was the incessant thumping from his head or the unwelcome and sudden intrusion of the streams of bright sunlight that burst in when the curtains were opened, but whatever, he jolted upwards in the bed, immediately put his hands to his throbbing temples, and only slowly was he able to prise his heavy eyelids apart.

As the world came into view, hazily at first, and then a little more clearly, he saw that Amanda was standing with her back to the bay window. She watched as he came to life and did not rush him; rather, she regarded him intently with an air of benevolent firmness, like a time-served matron.

She didn't otherwise look much like a middle-aged stereotypical matron, but the sight of her soothed his brain. He felt behind and puffed up the pillows and, folding his hands behind, propped up his head.

"How are you feeling?" she asked.

This enquiry provoked the return of the thumping between his ears. He conducted a quick audit of his body from top to toe.

"Sore and very stiff but okay otherwise, I think." He gave out a massive sneeze which shook his entire shell. It wasn't one of the normal morning wheezes either, and when it was followed in rapid succession by several more and accompanied by some involuntary snorting, he realised that he had a foul cold. He wasn't complaining, though. It seemed to be about the best possible result one could have hoped for under the circumstances.

At first, the events of last night were scrambled, but as his senses recovered, it all refocused in horrible detail. There could, he knew, be no forgetting. He had not even answered her bland enquiry, and she now walked toward him and sat on the bed very near him. "Here, drink this."

She leant down and picked up a mug from the floor beside her feet and, with its rising steam and her entreating manner, he concluded that it was some type of restorative preparation.

He took it and sipped it cautiously and, having decided that the cure was worse than the disease, replaced it on the adjacent table. But she stopped him. With a firm reassuring hand, she clasped his and returned the mug towards him.

He shut his eyes and squeezed her hand tightly. It felt so good to be near and to touch someone. Someone who he could trust and was alive. They sat in this position for some moments and then he said, "How did I get up here? I don't remember anything after ..." He hesitated a little and finished, "... after Hamish."

She did not answer and instead prised her hand from his grasp, leant across him and, without speaking, kissed him lightly on the forehead. "Later. Look, do you want to get up? I could make you some breakfast."

"I'll try."

She went out of the room, and a moment later, but not without difficulty, he swung his weary legs from under the duvet. After a short struggle, he forced himself up and across to the bay window. From the window, all outside was calm, even serene. The sun shone strongly, unhindered by the cloudless blue sky. In harmony, the sea was flat, deep blue and reassuringly calm, save for a very few white strips where it met the shore.

He wanted to try but it was not, and it never would be again, quite possible for his mood to match the scene, and his heart felt suddenly very heavy as he shuffled across to the bathroom.

As he walked, he realised that by spending the night in this room, their room, it had been the first time he had done so since her death, and as he entered the bathroom his eyes were drawn to her many accessories. He began to cry noiselessly and looked away quickly, focusing on showering and cleaning his teeth.

Having satisfactorily completed these ablutions, he found his body moved a little more freely and that he was hungry, so he quickly dressed and moved down the stairs and into the kitchen.

He ate. Amanda watched him and they did not speak until he was finished. "Do you want to talk?" she asked.

"Yes, okay."

They walked out of the door and down the drive.

"Where's the Volvo?" Jack asked.

"I had it taken away. We'll do a few tests."

"So, what's it all about, Amanda?"

She took his arm, led him forward and, in a clear and emotionless voice, began. "I waited up at the quarry. Do you remember that much?"

"Yes."

"Well, just after you left, the man you knocked out woke up with a very sore head. The police hadn't arrived, so I had a chat with him." She smiled a little wryly as she said this and continued. "He wasn't very talkative at first, but after a little while, I managed to get something out of him."

"Why would he talk to you?"

She said coldly, "I opened the car door, he saw Phillips, and I threatened to do the same to him if he didn't answer my questions."

"Would you have killed him?"

"No, and he called my bluff. Of course, he didn't care whether I killed him or not." She let this statement linger for a moment and then she explained. "They never do, you know. Some say they're crazy and mad. Just senseless psychopaths. But of course, they're not. In a way, in the best of them there's a terrible nobility. They give no quarter, but they ask none either." She mused as if recalling all such types she had encountered and, satisfied that there were few exceptions to this rule of thumb, confirmed, "Everyone of that type I've ever met."

"And do you meet many folks like that in the publishing world?"

Amanda laughed. "Oh, I don't do much publishing these days. In fact, you're my only client now."

"Not very lucrative," Jack said.

"No, it's not," she said. "Mostly I've been working for my father for a few years now."

"What is the family business?" Jack asked.

"Oh, government stuff. Security, that sort of thing." She didn't expand on that and continued talking about the events of last night. "Of course, all he cared about were the arms. So, I offered him a trade. The arms for the information."

"What information?"

"Who killed Marion and, of course, my sister."

"Your sister?"

"Yes, she was killed, in the line of duty you might say."

Jack stopped walking and looked at her desperately. He had so many questions now.

"I'll tell you the whole story later. Where were we? Oh yes, the man in the quarry and the deal."

If she didn't want to talk about that, it was up to her. Jack said, "But surely he wouldn't go for that? I mean, how could he believe you? How would he know that you would keep the bargain? And how could you do that? Surely the arms were what you were after?"

"Of course, he couldn't be sure of any of that, but he did know that I could arrange for the lorry to be intercepted, and besides, I was asking him for something that he could deliver. It wasn't something that would destroy his entire operation, and although he didn't want to do it, I had given him a real choice. The arms or his agent. The agent who had killed Marion and Murray. Of course, you see, if he was prepared to die for his cause then he didn't see why another volunteer shouldn't also. So, to save the arms shipment, he gave me the name."

Jack was bewildered. "He told you about Hamish?"

"Yes." She furrowed her brow and admitted, "I hadn't expected that, and for a moment, I didn't know what to do."

This first sign of fallibility was reassuring to him but her indecision had, it seemed, been only momentary. "But luckily the police arrived and I gave them a short account of most of the matter, made my excuses and left for the house."

"Did you tell them, the police, about the arms?"

She was unconcerned. "No."

"Isn't that a breach of duty?" Jack asked. "Surely you were meant to pick up the guns?"

Amanda said casually, "I've got a bit of discretion in my role. Anyway, I had made the deal, given my word."

"An interesting bargain."

"You see, it didn't really matter. About him, I mean. But with Marion and Jane it was personal. I cared nothing for him or the arms. Why should I? If I'd have killed him, someone else would have taken over, and, if we'd captured the guns, then they would just have got some more. It was more important to get the agent. For you, do you see?" She looked at him and added, "At least then, maybe, you'd have a chance to recover."

Jack protested. "Maybe, but you can't do that, surely?"

"Oh, well, I can."

She was a fully trained professional but she had a freelance mind. Such big decisions, so black or so white to her, would have taken him a lifetime to resolve.

"What then?" he asked.

"Well, nothing, really. I came down here, to the house, and burst in and there you were, drinking."

"Did you think you would find me dead?"

She didn't answer.

They had reached the end of the path as they had walked and conducted a short tour of the crumbling cottage. She looked over the cliff edge but Jack didn't.

"What will you do now?" she asked.

"Stay here. Finish the book maybe. What else?"

"I've spoken to the police. Marion's body can be released now. What do you want? Do you want me to handle things?"

Jack couldn't remember coming to a decision on this, but it seemed he had decided. "No, I'll get her back. There's a churchyard over there. I want her near me."

"When?"

"I'll speak to McCallum."

She said, "You want me to stay for a while, after the funeral?"

"Yes, I do, but I think I'm going to need some time on my own. I need to think, and I need to mourn. And so do you."

She took his hand. "If you struggle, phone me and I'll come up. Do you promise?"

He squeezed her hand. "Yes, I will."

The Quartermaster

Jack didn't know how long it would take him, and how much he was going to struggle. It was a scary and uncertain future, but at least he had one friend.

Adam Parish

The Quartermaster

Adam Parish

*Book 1 of the
Jack Edwards and Amanda Barratt
Mystery series*

Also by Adam Parish
*Parthian Shot (2)
Loose Ends (3)*

To sign up for offer, updates
and find out more about Adam Parish
visit our website www.adam-parish.com